In Loving
Memory

Also by Sally Emerson

Fiction

SECOND SIGHT

LISTENERS

FIRE CHILD

SEPARATION

HEAT

BROKEN BODIES

Non-fiction

A CELEBRATION OF BABIES (anthology)

THE NURSERY TREASURY (anthology)

BE MINE: AN ANTHOLOGY FOR LOVERS,
WEDDINGS AND EVER AFTER

NEW LIFE: AN ANTHOLOGY FOR PARENTHOOD

In Loving Memory

*An Anthology for Memorial Services,
Funerals and Just Getting By*

Edited by Sally Emerson

Little, Brown

To my mother and father
with love

LITTLE, BROWN

First published in Great Britain by Little, Brown in 2004
Reprinted 2004 (twice), 2005, 2006, 2007, 2010, 2011

Introduction and selection copyright © Sally Emerson 2004

Copyright of poems rests with authors and other rights holders as
cited in the acknowledgements on pages 223–31, which constitute an
extension of this copyright page

A CIP catalogue record for this book
is available from the British Library.

ISBN 978-0-316-72599-6

Typeset in Bembo by M Rules
Printed and bound in Great Britain by
Clays Ltd, St Ives plc

Little, Brown
An imprint of
Little, Brown Book Group
100 Victoria Embankment
London EC4Y 0DY

An Hachette UK Company
www.hachette.co.uk

www.littlebrown.co.uk

Contents

ℭ

Parting

℃

MISSING

REMEMBERING

THANKSGIVING

FACING ETERNITY

꽃

SEEING THE PATTERN

✿

INSPIRATION

LOVE'S POWER

FINDING PEACE

ℭ

HYMNS, PRAYERS AND READINGS

INTRODUCTION

It seems almost impossible. The very time we feel at our worst, when we have just lost someone we love, is also the time we have carefully to plan a funeral service which sums up and captures the spirit of the one who has died. Of course, some people have memorial services a good few weeks or months later, which allows time to think, but even then the planning demands subtlety and sympathy and a flash of brilliance. How else to do justice to a whole life?

Our secular age makes funeral and memorial services even more demanding for those who plan them. It is, after all, unsettling to hear a vicar or priest offer up the traditional Bible readings, prayers, hymns, eulogy and promise of heaven at the funeral of someone who, in fact, had absolutely no belief in traditional religion. The church or chapel gives dignity and sanctity to the immense event that is being marked, the ending of a life, yet there is an uneasy air of hypocrisy about the proceedings. There is a need for readings that can replace or at least augment the traditional and powerful religious ones. This anthology offers writing that has the power and beauty to provide both comfort and inspiration. Some religious writing is included, but there is much here that is not Christian in inspiration.

This is above all a poetry anthology, though it contains pieces of prose, and some hymns and prayers. People turn to poetry at times of deep emotion to try to understand their feelings. Collections of love poetry are legion. I very much want this anthology to help people at another time of strong, unravelling emotion.

There is an honesty in the poems that have become popular for memorial services in recent years. The rage of W. H. Auden's 'Funeral Blues', popularised in the film *Four Weddings and a Funeral*, which proclaims, 'Stop all the clocks, cut off the telephone . . . The stars are not wanted now; put out every one', does not defer to death but attacks it head on. This is raw grief and rage; something huge has happened, someone much loved has died and the poet does not wish to muffle his grief with platitudes. The same mood of honesty is apparent in Edna St Vincent Millay's 'Dirge without Music', which states, 'I am not resigned to the shutting away of loving hearts in the hard ground . . . Elegant and curled/Is the blossom. Fragrant is the blossom. I know. But I do not approve./More precious was the light in your eyes than all the roses in the world.' The finest poetry should uplift not necessarily by offering words of comfort, but by expressing the truth in the best words possible. The agonised poems of Gerard Manley Hopkins encapsulate the real pain so many go through, and must help those who suffer to understand their suffering and to know that they are not alone.

Great poets and writers again and again glorify the beauty and splendour of the natural world. I wanted this anthology to celebrate life as well as dealing with death; after all, that someone has lived is something to be immensely grateful for. I particularly like Thomas Traherne's 'Thanksgivings for the Body', which offers praise to God 'From the framing of a needle's eye,/To the building of a tower:/From the squaring of trees,/To the polishing of kings' crowns . . . For all the mysteries, engines, instruments, wherewith the world is/filled, which we are able to frame and use to Thy glory.'

The popularity of 'Do Not Stand at My Grave and Weep' suggests a respect for nature, a modern pantheism that worships nature rather than God. The poem reminds mourners that the person they grieve for has become one with nature: 'I am a thousand winds that blow./I am the diamond glints on snow . . . When you awaken in the morning's hush/I am the swift uplifting rush/Of quiet birds in circled flight'. It is anonymous, but has been attributed to a number of people at different times, most recently to Stephen Cummins, a soldier killed in Northern Ireland, who left a copy for his relatives. In his elegy on the death of Keats, 'Adonais', Shelley explored the idea of the dead person being absorbed into nature: 'there is heard/His voice in all her music, from the moan/Of thunder, to the song of night's sweet bird . . . He is a portion of the loveliness/Which once he made more lovely . . .'

The anonymous 'She Is Gone', which prefaced the order of service at Westminster Abbey for the Queen Mother's funeral, is not a great poem but does encourage the reader to rejoice in a life lived, rather than letting despair take its fierce grip. It very directly reminds us to look forward, to cherish her memory: 'You can close your eyes and pray that she'll come back/or you can open your eyes and see all she's left . . . You can cry and close your mind, be empty and turn your back/or you can do what she'd want: smile, open your eyes, love and go on.' While Noël Coward pointed out that he would like to be 'missed a bit', something we all feel, Joyce Grenfell gaily announced, 'Weep if you must/Parting is hell,/But life goes on,/So sing as well.'

One of the most moving pieces of writing here is just a few sentences from the novel *Captain Corelli's Mandolin*. The old doctor Iannis advised Captain Corelli who has seen his companions die violently: 'When loved ones die, you have to live on their behalf. See things as though with their eyes. Remember how they used to say things, and use those words oneself. Be thankful that you can do things that they cannot, and also feel the sadness of it. This is how I live without Pelagia's mother. I have no interest in flowers, but for her I will look at a rock-rose or a lily. For her I eat aubergines, because she loved them.' The theme of memory and of people living on through memory, is very much a part of this anthology. As Samuel Butler said, 'To die completely, a person must not only forget but be forgotten, and he who is not forgotten is not dead.' Brian Patten's 'So Many Different Lengths of Time' also explores this idea: 'A man lives for as long as we carry him inside us,/for as long as we carry the harvest of his dreams,/for as long as we ourselves live,/holding memories in common, a man lives.'

Perhaps the greatest consolation is love, whether we call God nature, or nature God, or love God, or God love. Thornton Wilder's thoughts in 'The Bridge of San Luis Rey' have become famous since Tony Blair read them out after the Twin Towers disaster, pointing out that there is a land of the living and a land of the dead, and that the bridge is love, 'The only survival, the only meaning'. The lines which were read out from a poem by Henry van Dyke at Princess Diana's funeral include the words: 'For those who love, time is Eternity.'

In the last section I have included a few favourite hymns and prayers. Some will be moved by the old hymns they have heard all their lives, either because they are religious themselves or simply because of the comfort of tradition. But many people will wish to play pieces of music of particular importance to the deceased or the mourners. Popular choices include Simon and Garfunkel's 'Bridge over Troubled Water'; 'Knocking on Heaven's Door' recorded by artists including Bob Dylan and Eric Clapton; 'Tears in Heaven', written and recorded by Eric Clapton after the death of his young son; 'Yesterday' by the Beatles; 'Imagine' by John Lennon; and 'New Morning' and 'If Not for You' by Bob Dylan. My mother and father, reprobates that they are, want Peggy Lee's 'Is That All There Is?' and Lynn Anderson's 'I Never Promised You a Rose Garden'.

One of the most popular passages for memorial services included here is by Henry Scott-Holland, which announces: 'Death is nothing at all./I have only slipped away into the next room./I am I and you are you./Whatever we were to each other,/that we are still . . . /Why should I be out of mind/because I am out of sight?/I am waiting for you for an interval./Somewhere very near, just/around the corner./All is well.' Those who are not religious, and do not believe in heaven, might be uneasy with this passage, but there is a kernel of indisputable truth in it. While you remember that person, they still exist in a way.

My view is, whatever gets you through the night: we should all find comfort where we can. The chances of any individual turning up on earth are tiny. Anyone who has lived or is living has already beaten incredible odds to be on this glorious planet. We should all rejoice that those who have died have lived.

SALLY EMERSON

RAGE

Do Not Go Gentle into that Good Night

Do not go gentle into that good night,
Old age should burn and rave at close of day;
Rage, rage against the dying of the light.

Though wise men at their end know dark is right,
Because their words had forked no lightning they
Do not go gentle into that good night.

Good men, the last wave by, crying how bright
Their frail deeds might have danced in a green bay,
Rage, rage against the dying of the light.

Wild men who caught and sang the sun in flight,
And learn, too late, they grieved it on its way,
Do not go gentle into that good night.

Grave men, near death, who see with blinding sight
Blind eyes could blaze like meteors and be gay,
Rage, rage against the dying of the light.

And you, my father, there on the sad height,
Curse, bless, me now with your fierce tears, I pray.
Do not go gentle into that good night.
Rage, rage against the dying of the light.

DYLAN THOMAS (1914–53)

Funeral Blues

Stop all the clocks, cut off the telephone,
Prevent the dog from barking with a juicy bone,
Silence the pianos, and with muffled drum
Bring out the coffin, let the mourners come.

Let aeroplanes circle moaning overhead
Scribbling on the sky the message He is Dead,
Put crêpe bows round the white necks of the public doves,
Let the traffic policemen wear black cotton gloves.

He was my North, my South, my East and West,
My working week and my Sunday rest,
My noon, my midnight, my talk, my song;
I thought love could last for ever: I was wrong.

The stars are not wanted now: put out every one;
Pack up the moon and dismantle the sun;
Pour away the ocean and sweep up the wood;
For nothing now can ever come to any good.

W. H. AUDEN (1907–73)

Dirge without Music

I am not resigned to the shutting away of loving
    hearts in the hard ground.
So it is, and so it will be, for so it has been, time out
    of mind:
Into the darkness they go, the wise and the lovely.
    Crowned
With lilies and with laurel they go; but I am not
    resigned.

Lovers and thinkers, into the earth with you.
Be one with the dull, the indiscriminate dust.
A fragment of what you felt, of what you knew,
A formula, a phrase remains, – but the best is lost.

The answers quick and keen, the honest look, the
    laughter, the love, –
They are gone. They are gone to feed the roses.
    Elegant and curled
Is the blossom. Fragrant is the blossom. I know. But I
    do not approve.
More precious was the light in your eyes than all the
    roses in the world.

Down, down, down into the darkness of the grave
Gently they go, the beautiful, the tender, the kind;
Quietly they go, the intelligent, the witty, the brave.
I know. But I do not approve. And I am not resigned.

EDNA ST VINCENT MILLAY (1892–1950)

11

Flesh of My Flesh

Children of my children's children
And beyond;
Now, well into
The tragi-
  comic
    slide
Of my flesh into decay,
I yearn for you.

I long for:
Lush, languid babies
  laughing in the sunlight;
Gawky, gap-toothed children,
  gambolling into life;
Adolescents, sprouting breasts
and beards,
  with equal mix of secret shame
  and pride;
Lovers not quite willing to believe
  in your astounding luck;
Newly-minted parents,
  wonder-filled and worshipful
  with awe.

Not for me
The all too certain maladies
Of
  your
    flesh.
The sleepless nights,

The screams of rage and pain,
The heart-stopping
  sickness

and
accidents.
I did that once and more,
Paying just dues
To Life
For her great gift to us.
But for you who will be born
When my flesh is almost finished,
Or dissolved,
I lust only for the joy.

And if perchance
One of you,
Courteous, or curious, or both,
Should visit at my cool,
indifferent grave,
It is my passion
That you know
That as I write to you:
    I fiddle with the texture of my hair
    And gaze upon a limpid grove
    Of trees
    And feel the after-glow of a
        warm and sunny day,

Just as you do, my darlings,
Just exactly
        as
            you
                do.

I write to you, ghostly little loves,
Present only in the loins and longings
Of your ancestors,
Not to lecture you
That you are dust

And unto dust you will return,
(Though lectures I have heard)
Nor to ask that you should theorize
On spiritual and fleshly love,
(Though theories I do know)
Nor even to tell you that life is good,
(For there are some of you
who think that,
And others who do not)
But simply to let you know,
(Though why I care I do not know)
That just as real as is the drop of sweat
Now running down my side,
In whose existence you will scarce
believe,
I was real once.
I was very real.

BARBARA BOGGS SIGMUND (1939–90)

from One Who Stays

How empty seems the town now you are gone!
　　A wilderness of sad streets, where gaunt walls
　　Hide nothing to desire; sunshine falls
Eery, distorted, as it long had shone
On white, dead faces tombed in halls of stone.
　　The whir of motors, stricken through with calls
　　Of playing boys, floats up at intervals;
But all these noises blur to one long moan.
　　What quest is worth pursuing? And how strange
That other men still go accustomed ways!
I hate their interest in the things they do.
　　A spectre-horde repeating without change.

AMY LOWELL (1874–1925)

On the Eve of His Execution

My prime of youth is but a frost of cares,
My feast of joy is but a dish of pain,
My crop of corn is but a field of tares,
And all my good is but vain hope of gain;
The day is past, and yet I saw no sun,
And now I live, and now my life is done.

My tale was heard and yet it was not told,
My fruit is fallen and yet my leaves are green,
My youth is spent and yet I am not old,
I saw the world and yet I was not seen;
My thread is cut and yet it is not spun,
And now I live, and now my life is done.

I sought my death and found it in my womb,
I looked for life and found it was a shade,
I trod the earth and knew it was my tomb,
And now I die, and now I was but made;
My glass is full, and now my glass is run,
And now I live, and now my life is done.

CHIDIOCK TICHBORNE (c.1558–86)

Last Words

'God bless . . . God damn.'

JAMES THURBER
(1894–1961)

GRIEF

No Worst, There Is None

No worst, there is none. Pitched past pitch of grief,
More pangs will, schooled at forepangs, wilder wring.
Comforter, where, where is your comforting?
Mary, mother of us, where is your relief?
My cries heave, herds-long, huddle in the main, a chief
Woe, world-sorrow; on an age-old anvil wince and sing –
Then lull, then leave off. Fury had shrieked 'No ling-
ering! Let me be fell: force I must be brief.

    O the mind, mind has mountains; cliffs of fall
Frightful, sheer, no-man-fathomed. Hold them cheap
May who ne'er hung there. Nor does long our small
Durance deal with that steep or deep. Here! creep,
Wretch, under a comfort serves in a whirlwind: all
Life death does end and each day dies with sleep.

GERARD MANLEY HOPKINS (1844–89)

from The Rebecca Notebook

The old adage, Time heals all wounds, is only true if there is no suppuration within. To be bitter, to lament unceasingly, 'Why did this have to happen to him?' makes the wound fester; the mind, renewing the stab, causes the wound to bleed afresh. It is hard, very hard, not to be bitter in the early days, not to blame doctors, hospitals, drugs, that failed to cure. Harder still for the woman whose husband died not by illness but by accident, who was cut short in full vigour, in the prime of life, killed perhaps in a car crash returning home from work. The first instinct is to seek revenge upon the occupants of the other car, themselves unhurt, whose selfish excess of speed caused the disaster. Yet this is no answer to grief. All anger, all reproach, turns inwards upon itself. The infection spreads, pervading the mind and body.

I would say to those who mourn – and I can only speak from my own experience – look upon each day that comes as a challenge, as a test of courage. The pain will come in waves, some days worse than others, for no apparent reason. Accept the pain. Do not suppress it. Never attempt to hide grief from yourself. Little by little, just as the deaf, the blind, the handicapped develop with time an extra sense to balance disability, so the bereaved, the widowed, will find new strength, new vision, born of the very pain and loneliness which seem, at first, impossible to master. I address myself more especially to the middle-aged who, like myself, look back to over thirty years or more of married life and find it hardest to adapt. The young must, of their very nature, heal sooner than ourselves.

DAPHNE DU MAURIER (1907–89)

After Great Pain

After great pain, a formal feeling comes –
The Nerves sit ceremonious, like Tombs –
The stiff Heart questions was it He, that bore,
And Yesterday, or Centuries before?

The Feet, mechanical, go round –
Of Ground, or Air, or Ought –
A Wooden way
Regardless grown,
A Quartz contentment, like a stone –

This is the Hour of Lead –
Remembered, if outlived,
As Freezing persons, recollect the Snow –
First – Chill – then Stupor – then the letting go –

EMILY DICKINSON (1830–86)

I Wake and Feel the Fell of Dark

I wake and feel the fell of dark, not day.
What hours, O what black hours we have spent
This night! what sights you, heart, saw; ways you went!
And more must, in yet longer light's delay.
    With witness I speak this. But where I say
Hours I mean years, mean life. And my lament
Is cries countless, cries like dead letters sent
To dearest him that lives alas! away.

I am gall, I am heartburn. God's most deep decree
Bitter would have me taste: my taste was me;
Bones built in me, flesh filled, blood brimmed with curse.
Selfyeast of spirit a dull dough sours. I see
The lost are like this, and their scourge to be
As I am mine, their sweating selves; but worse.

GERARD MANLEY HOPKINS (1844–89)

from In Memoriam

Dark house, by which once more I stand
   Here in the unlovely street,
   Doors, where my heart was used to beat
So quickly, waiting for a hand,

A hand that can be clasp'd no more –
   Behold me, for I cannot sleep,
   And like a guilty thing I creep
At earliest morning to the door.

He is not here; but far away
   The noise of life begins again,
   And ghastly thro' the drizzling rain
On the bald street breaks the blank day.

ALFRED, LORD TENNYSON (1809–92)

After the Burial

Yes, faith is a goodly anchor;
When skies are sweet as a psalm,
At the bows it lolls so stalwart,
In its bluff, broad-shouldered calm.

And when over breakers to leeward
The tattered surges are hurled,
It may keep our head to the tempest,
With its grip on the base of the world.

But, after the shipwreck, tell me
What help in its iron thews,
Still true to the broken hawser,
Deep down among seaweed and ooze?

In the breaking gulfs of sorrow,
When the helpless feet stretch out
And find in the deeps of darkness
No footing so solid as doubt,

Then better one spar of Memory,
One broken plank of the Past,
That our human heart may cling to,
Though hopeless of shore at last!

To the spirit its splendid conjectures,
To the flesh its sweet despair,
Its tears o'er the thin-worn locket
With its anguish of deathless hair!

Immortal? I feel it and know it,
Who doubts it of such as she?
But that is the pang's very secret, –
Immortal away from me.

There's a narrow ridge in the graveyard
Would scarce stay a child in his race,
But to me and my thought it is wider
Than the star-sown vague of Space.

Your logic, my friend, is perfect,
Your morals most drearily true;
But, since the earth clashed on *her* coffin,
I keep hearing that, and not you.

Console if you will, I can bear it;
'Tis a well-meant alms of breath;
But not all the preaching since Adam
Has made Death other than Death.

It is pagan; but wait till you feel it, –
That jar of our earth, that dull shock
When the ploughshare of deeper passion
Tears down to our primitive rock.

Communion in spirit! Forgive me,
But I, who am earthy and weak,
Would give all my incomes from dreamland
For a touch of her hand on my cheek.

That little shoe in the corner,
So worn and wrinkled and brown,
With its emptiness confutes you
And argues your wisdom down.

JAMES RUSSELL LOWELL (1819–91)

from A Grief Observed

No one ever told me that grief felt so like fear. I am not afraid, but the sensation is like being afraid. The same fluttering in the stomach, the same restlessness, the yawning. I keep on swallowing.

At other times it feels like being mildly drunk, or concussed. There is a sort of invisible blanket between the world and me. I find it hard to take in what anyone says. Or perhaps, hard to want to take it in. It is so uninteresting. Yet I want the others to be about me. I dread the moments when the house is empty. If only they would talk to one another and not to me.

There are moments, most unexpectedly, when something inside me tries to assure me that I don't really mind so much, not so very much, after all. Love is not the whole of a man's life. I was happy before I ever met H. I've plenty of what are called 'resources'. People get over these things. Come, I shan't do so badly. One is ashamed to listen to this voice but it seems for a little to be making out a good case. Then comes a sudden jab of red-hot memory and all this 'commonsense' vanishes like and ant in the mouth of a furnace . . .

Meanwhile, where is God? This is one of the most disquieting symptoms. When you are happy, so happy that you have no sense of needing Him, so happy that you are tempted to feel His claims upon you as an interruption, if you remember yourself and turn to Him with gratitude and praise, you will be – or so it feels – welcomed with open arms. But go to Him when your need is desperate, when all other help is vain, and what do you find? A door slammed in your face, and a sound of bolting and doubling bolting on the inside. After that, silence. You may as well turn away. The longer you wait, the more emphatic the silence will become. There are no lights in the windows. It might be an empty house. Was it ever inhabited? It seemed so once. And that seeming was as strong as this. What can this mean? Why is He so present a commander in our time of prosperity and so very absent a help in time of trouble?

C. S. Lewis (1898–1963)

Save Me

Save me, O God: for the waters are come in even unto my soul.

I stick fast in the deep mire, where no ground is: I am come into deep waters, so that the floods run over me.

I am weary of crying: my throat is dry: my sight faileth me for waiting so long upon my God . . .

Take me out of the mire, that I sink not: O let me be delivered from them that hate me, and out of the deep waters.

Let not the water-flood drown me, neither let the deep swallow me up: and let not the pit shut her mouth upon me.

Hear me, O Lord, for thy loving-kindness is comfortable: turn thee unto me according to the multitude of thy mercies.

PSALM 69: 1–3, 15–17

from Perfect Happiness

Loss clamped her every morning as she woke; it sat its grinding weight on her and rode her, like the old man of the sea. It roared in her ears when people talked to her so that frequently she did not hear what they said. It interrupted her when she spoke, so that she faltered in mid-sentence, lost track. A little less, now; remissions came and went. The days stalked by, taking her with them . . .

During the early days and weeks of her solitude Frances had come to realise that grief like illness is unstable; it ebbs and flows in tides, it steals away to a distance then comes roaring back, it torments by deception. It plays games with time and with reality. On some mornings she would wake and Steven's presence was so distant and yet so reassuring that she thought herself purged; he seemed both absent and present, she felt close to him and at the same time freed, she thought that at last she was walking alone. And then, within hours she would be back once more in that dark trough: incredulous, raging, ground into her misery. Time, that should be linear, had become formless; mercurial and unreliable, it took her away from the moment of Steven's death and then flung her back beside it.

PENELOPE LIVELY (1933–)

from Antony and Cleopatra

ACT IV, SCENE XV

O, wither'd is the garland of the war,
The soldier's pole is fall'n: young boys and girls
Are level now with men: the odds is gone,
And there is nothing left remarkable
Beneath the visiting moon.

WILLIAM SHAKESPEARE (1564–1616)

Musée des Beaux Arts

About suffering they were never wrong,
The Old Masters: how well they understood
Its human position; how it takes place
While someone else is eating or opening a window or just
    walking dully along;
How, when the aged are reverently, passionately waiting
For the miraculous birth, there always must be
Children who did not specially want it to happen, skating
On a pond at the edge of the wood:
They never forgot
That even the dreadful martyrdom must run its course
Anyhow in a corner, some untidy spot
Where the dogs go on with their doggy life and the
    torturer's horse
Scratches its innocent behind on a tree.

In Brueghel's *Icarus*, for instance: how everything turns away
Quite leisurely from the disaster; the ploughman may
Have heard the splash, the forsaken cry,
But for him it was not an important failure; the sun shone
As it had to on the white legs disappearing into the green
Water; and the expensive delicate ship that must have seen
Something amazing, a boy falling out of the sky,
Had somewhere to get to and sailed calmly on.

W. H. AUDEN (1907–73)

from On the Beach at Night

Weep not, child,
Weep not, my darling,
With these kisses let me remove your tears,
The ravening clouds shall not long be victorious,
They shall not long possess the sky, they devour
      the stars only in apparition,
Jupiter shall emerge, be patient, watch again
      another night, the Pleiades shall emerge,
They are immortal, all those stars both silvery
      and golden shall shine out again,
The great stars and the little ones shall shine out
      again, they endure.
The vast immortal suns and the long-enduring
      pensive moons shall again shine.

WALT WHITMAN (1819–92)

from Rebecca

When people suffer a great shock, like death, or the loss of a limb, I believe they don't feel it just at first. If your hand is taken from you, you don't know, for a few minutes, that your hand is gone. You go on feeling the fingers. You stretch and beat them on the air, one by one, and all the time there is nothing there, no hand, no fingers . . . I was shocked at my lack of emotion and this queer cold absence of distress. Little by little the feeling will come back to me, I said to myself, little by little I shall understand.

DAPHNE DU MAURIER (1907–89)

The Suicides

It is hard for us to enter
the kind of despair they must have known
and because it is hard we must get in by breaking
the lock if necessary for we have not the key,
though for them there was no lock and the surrounding walls
were supple, receiving as waves, and they drowned
though not lovingly; it is we only
who must enter in this way.

Temptations will beset us, once we are in.
We may want to catalogue what they have stolen.
We may feel suspicion; we may even criticise the decor
of their suicidal despair, may perhaps feel
it was incongruously comfortable.

Knowing the temptations then
let us go in
deep to their despair and their skin and know
they died because words they had spoken
returned always homeless to them.

JANET FRAME (1924–2004)

The Stag Cries

In all the world
There is no way whatever.
The stag cries even
In the most remote mountain.

THE PRIEST
FUJIWARA NO TOSHINARI

from A Letter to a Friend
on the Death of His Mother

19 NOVEMBER 1891

May I try to tell you again where your only comfort lies? It is not in forgetting the happy past. People bring us well-meant but miserable consolations when they tell us what time will do to help our grief. We do not want to lose our grief, because our grief is bound up with our love and we could not cease to mourn without being robbed of our affections.

PHILLIPS BROOKS (1835–93)

from A Letter to David Garnett

Don't think I am unhappy and alone . . . I am in a new country and she is the compass I travel by . . .

I was grateful to you for your letter after Valentine's death, for you were the sole person who said that for pain and loneliness there is no cure. I suppose people have not the moral stamina to contemplate the idea of no cure, and to ease their uneasiness they trot out the most astonishing placebos. I was assured I would find consolation in writing, in gardening, in tortoises, in tapestry . . . in keeping bees, in social service . . . and many of these consolers were people whom I had previously found quite rational. Your only runner-up was Reynolds Stone's wife, who said whisky . . . But when one has had one's head cut off . . .

SYLVIA TOWNSEND WARNER (1893–1978)

from A Grief Observed

An odd by-product of my loss is that I'm aware of being an embarrassment to everyone I meet. At work, at the club, in the street, I see people, as they approach me, trying to make up their minds whether they'll 'say something about it' or not. I hate it if they do, and if they don't. Some funk it altogether. R. has been avoiding me for a week. I like best the well-brought-up young men, almost boys, who walk up to me as if I were a dentist, turn very red, get it over, and then edge away to the bar as quickly as they decently can. Perhaps the bereaved ought to be isolated in special settlements like lepers.

To some I'm worse than an embarrassment. I am a death's head. Whenever I meet a happily married pair I can feel them both thinking. 'One or other of us must some day be as he is now.'

C. S. LEWIS (1898–1963)

Advice on Low Spirits

TO LADY GEORGIANA MORPETH,
16 FEBRUARY 1820

Dear Lady Georgiana,

Nobody has suffered more from low spirits than I have done, so I feel for you.
1. Live as well and drink as much wine as you dare. 2. Go in the shower-bath with a small quantity of water at a temperature low enough to give you a slight sensation of cold – 75 or 80. 3. Amusing books. 4. Short views of human life not farther than dinner or tea. 5. Be as busy as you can. 6. See as much as you can of those friends who respect and like you. 7. And of those acquaintances who amuse you. 8. Make no secret of low spirits to your friends but talk of them fully: they are always the worse for dignified concealment. 9. Attend to the effects tea and coffee produce upon you. 10. Compare your lot with that of other people. 11. Don't expect too much of human life, a sorry business at best. 12. Avoid poetry, dramatic representations (except comedy), music, serious novels, melancholy sentimental people, and everything likely to excite feeling or emotion not ending in active benevolence. 13. Do good and endeavour to please everybody of every degree. 14. Be as much as you can in the open air without fatigue. 15. Make the room where you commonly sit gay and pleasant. 16. Struggle little by little against idleness. 17. Don't be too severe upon yourself, but do yourself justice. 18. Keep good, blazing fires. 19. Be firm and constant in the exercise of rational religion. 20. Believe me dear Lady Georgiana very truly yours,

SYDNEY SMITH (1771–1845)

The Ring

King Solomon asked his wisest men for something that would make him happy when he was sad, but also sad when he was happy. They consulted and came back with a ring engraved with the words 'This too will pass'.

ANONYMOUS

from Nature

Nature always wears the colors of the spirit. To a man laboring under calamity, the heat of his own fire hath sadness in it. Then there is a kind of contempt of the landscape felt by him who has just lost by death a dear friend. The sky is less grand as it shuts down over less worth in the population.

RALPH WALDO EMERSON (1803–82)

from Ross

I will not insult you by trying to tell you that one day you will forget. I know as well as you that you will not. But, at least, in time you will not remember as fiercely as you do now – and I pray that that time may be soon.

TERENCE RATTIGAN (1911–77)

from The Duchess of Malfi

ACT IV, SCENE I

Look you, the stars shine still.

JOHN WEBSTER (c. 1580–c. 1634)

from Cranford

One gives people in grief their own way.

ELIZABETH CLEGHORN GASKELL
(1810–65)

from De Profundis

There are times when sorrow seems to be the only truth.

OSCAR WILDE (1854–1900)

Wrong

It is wrong to sorrow without ceasing.

HOMER (?8th century BC)

PARTING

Taking Leave of a Friend

Blue mountains to the north of the walls,
White river winding about them;
Here we must make separation
And go out through a thousand miles of dead grass.
Mind like a floating wide cloud,
Sunset like the parting of old acquaintances
Who bow over their clasped hands at a distance.
Our horses neigh to each other
               as we are departing.

                    EZRA POUND (1885–1972)
                       from the Chinese

Old Gaelic Blessing

May the road rise to meet you.
May the wind be always at your back.
May the sun shine warm upon your face.
May the rains fall softly upon your fields until we meet again.
May God hold you in the hollow of his hand.

ANONYMOUS

Ode to My Brother

By ways remote and distant waters sped,
Brother, to thy sad grave-side am I come,
That I may give the last gifts to the dead
And vainly parley with thine ashes dumb;
Since she who now bestows and now denies
Hath taken thee, hapless brother, from mine eyes.

But lo! these gifts, the heirlooms of past years,
Are made sad things to grace thy coffin shell,
Take them, all drenched with a brother's tears,
And, brother, for all time, hail and farewell.

CATULLUS (*c.*84–*c.*54 BC)

Turn Again

Read at Princess Diana's funeral by her eldest sister.

If I should die and leave you here awhile,
Be not like others, sore undone, who keep
Long vigils by silent dust, and weep.
For my sake, turn again to life and smile,
Nerving thy heart and trembling hand to do
Something to comfort weaker hearts than thine.
Complete these dear unfinished tasks of mine
And I perchance may therein comfort you!

MARY LEE HALL

The Parting Glass

Oh all the time that e'er I spent,
I spent it in good company;
And any harm that e'er I've done,
I trust it was to none but me;
May those I've loved through all the years
Have memories now they'll e'er recall;
So fill to me the parting glass,
Goodnight, and joy be with you all.

Oh all the comrades that e'er I had,
Are sorry for my going away;
And all the loved ones that e'er I had
Would wish me one more day to stay.
But since it falls unto my lot
That I should leave and you should not,
I'll gently rise and I'll softly call
Goodnight, and joy be with you all.

Of all good times that e'er we shared,
I leave to you fond memory;
And for all the friendship that e'er we had
I ask you to remember me;
And when you sit and stories tell,
I'll be with you and help recall;
So fill to me the parting glass,
God bless, and joy be with you all.

Irish Traditional

from Hymen

Never more will the wind
Cherish you again,
Never more will the rain.

Never more
Shall we find you bright
In the snow and wind.

The snow is melted,
The snow is gone,
And you are flown:

Like a bird out of our hand,
Like a light out of our heart,
You are gone.

H.D. (HILDA DOOLITTLE)
(1886–1961)

from Delia Elena San Marco

We said goodbye at the corner of Eleventh. From the other sidewalk I turned to look back; you too had turned, and you waved goodbye to me.

A river of vehicles and people was flowing between us. It was five o'clock on an ordinary afternoon. How was I to know that that river was Acheron the doleful, the insuperable?

We did not see each other again, and a year later you were dead.

And now I seek out that memory and look at it, and I think it was false, and that behind that trivial farewell was infinite separation.

Last night I stayed in after dinner and reread, in order to understand these things, the last teaching Plato put in his master's mouth. I read that the soul may escape when the flesh dies.

And now I do not know whether the truth is in the ominous subsequent interpretation, or in the unsuspecting farewell.

For if souls do not die, it is right that we should not make much of saying goodbye.

To say goodbye to each other is to deny separation. It is like saying, 'Today we play at separating, but we will see each other tomorrow.' Man invented farewells because he somehow knows he is immortal, even though he may seem gratuitous and ephemeral.

Sometime, Delia, we will take up again – beside what river? – this uncertain dialogue, and we will ask each other if ever, in a city lost on a plain, we were Borges and Delia.

JORGE LUIS BORGES (1899–1986)

Grey Evening

When you went, how was it you carried with you
My missal book of fine, flamboyant hours?
My book of turrets and of red-thorn bowers,
And skies of gold, and ladies in bright tissue?

Now underneath a blue-grey twilight, heaped
Beyond the withering snow of the shorn fields
Stands rubble of stunted houses; all is reaped
And garnered that the golden daylight yields.

Now lamps like yellow echoes glimmer among
The shadowy stubble of the under-dusk;
As farther off the scythe of night is swung
Ripe little stars come rolling from their husk.

And all the earth is gone into a dust
Of greyness mingled with a fume of gold,
Time as branching lichens, pale as must,
Since all the sky has withered and gone cold.

And so I sit and scan the book of grey,
Feeling the shadows like a blind man reading,
All the fearful lest I find the last words bleeding:
Nay, take this weary Book of Hours away.

D. H. Lawrence (1885–1930)

After I Have Gone

Speak my name softly after I have gone.
I loved the quiet things, the flowers and the dew,
Field mice; birds homing; and the frost that shone
On nursery windows when my years were few;
And autumn mists subduing hill and plain
and blurring outlines of those older moods
that follow, after loss and grief and pain –
And last and best, a gentle laugh with friends,
All bitterness foregone, and evening near.
If we be kind and faithful when day ends,
We shall not meet that ragged starveling 'fear'
As one by one we take the unknown way –
Speak my name softly – there's no more to say –

VERA I. ARLETT (1896–1948)

Epitaph Upon a Child That Died

Here she lies, a pretty bud,
Lately made of flesh and blood:
Who as soon fell fast asleep
As her little eyes did peep.
Give her strewings, but not stir
The earth that lightly covers her.

Robert Herrick (1591–1674)

P'u – Hua Fei Hua

A flower and not a flower; of mist yet not of mist;
At midnight she was there; she went as daylight shone.
She came and for a little while was like a dream of spring,
And then, as morning clouds that vanish traceless,
     she was gone.

Po Chü-i (772–846)

On My First Son

Farewell, thou child of my right hand, and joy;
  My sin was too much hope of thee, lov'd boy.
Seven years thou wert lent to me, and I thee pay,
  Exacted by thy fate, on the just day.
Oh, could I lose all father now! For why
  Will man lament the state he should envy?
To have so soon 'scaped world's and flesh's rage,
  And if no other misery, yet age!
Rest in soft peace, and, asked, say, Here doth lie
  Ben Jonson his best piece of poetry.
For whose sake henceforth all his vows be such
  As what he loves may never like too much.

BEN JONSON (1572–1637)

Elegy

That one should leave the greenwood suddenly
In the good comrade-time of youth,
And clothed in the first coat of truth
Set out alone on an uncharted sea.

Who'll ever know what star
Summoned him, what mysterious shell
Locked in his ear that music and that spell,
And what grave ship was waiting for him there?

The greenwood empties soon of leaf and song.
Truth turns to pain. Our coats grow sere.
Barren the comings and goings on this shore.
He anchors off the Island of the Young.

GEORGE MACKAY BROWN (1921–96)

Always With You

Your mother is always with you.
She's the whisper of the leaves
as you walk down the street.
She's the smell of bleach
in your freshly laundered socks.
She's the cool hand on your brow
When you're not well.
Your mother lives inside your laughter.
She's crystallized in every teardrop.
She's the place you came from,
your first home.
She's the map you follow
with every step that you take.
She's your first love
and your first heartbreak . . .
and nothing on earth can separate you.

ANONYMOUS

Early Death

She passed away like morning dew
Before the sun was high;
So brief her time, she scarcely knew
The meaning of a sigh.

As round the rose its soft perfume,
Sweet love around her floated;
Admired she grew – while mortal doom
Crept on, unfeared, unnoted.

Love was her guardian Angel here,
But Love to Death resigned her;
Though Love was kind, why should we fear
But holy Death is kinder?

HARTLEY COLERIDGE (1796–1849)

My Life Closed Twice

My life closed twice before its close;
   It yet remains to see
If Immortality unveil
   A third event to me,

So huge, so hopeless to conceive,
   As these that twice befell.
Parting is all we know of heaven,
   And all we need of hell.

EMILY DICKINSON (1830–86)

Only a Little While

We were together
Only a little while,
And we believed our love
Would last a thousand years.

YAKAMOCHI (*c.*716–785)

Tableau Vivant

They think it's easy to be dead, those
who walk the pathway here in stylish shoes,
portable radios strapped to their arms,
selling the world's perishables, even
love songs. They think you just lie down
into dreams you will never tell anyone.
They don't know we still have plans, a yen
for romance, and miss things like hats
and casseroles.

As for dreams, we take up where the living
leave off. We like especially those
in which the dreamer is about to
fall over a cliff or from a bridge that
is falling too. We're only too glad
to look down on the river gorge enlarging
under a body's sudden weight, to have the ground
rushing up instead of this slow
caving in. We thrive in living out
the last precious memories of someone escaped
back into the morning light.

Occasionally there's a message saying they want
one of us back, someone out there
feeling guilt about a word or deed
that seems worse because we took it as
a living harm, then died
with it, quietly. But we know a lot about
forgiveness and we always make these trips with
a certain missionary zeal. We get back
into our old sad clothes. We stand again
at the parting, full of wronged tenderness and
needing a shave or a hairdo. We tell them
things are okay, not to waste their lives

in remorse, we never held it
against them, so much happens that one means.

But sometimes one of us gets stubborn, thinks
of evening the score. We leave them calling
after us, Sorry, Sorry, Sorry, and we don't
look back.

TESS GALLAGHER (1943–)

To Those I Love

If I should ever leave you whom I love
To go along the silent way,
Grieve not,
Nor speak of me with tears,
But laugh and talk of me as if I were beside
you there.

(I'd come – I'd come, could I but find a way!
But would not tears and grief be barriers?)
And when you hear a song
Or see a bird I loved,
Please do not let the thought of me be sad . . .
For I am loving you just as I always have . . .
You were so good to me!

There are so many things I wanted still to do –

So many things to say to you . . .
Remember that I did not fear . . .
It was just leaving you that was so hard to
face . . .
We cannot see beyond . . .
But this I know:
I love you so –

'twas heaven here with you!

ISLA PASCHAL RICHARDSON (1886–1971)

from Cancer Ward

But now . . . he remembered how the old folk used to die back home on the Kama – Russians, Tartars, Votyaks, or whatever they were. They didn't puff themselves up or fight against it and brag that they weren't going to die – they took death *calmly*. They didn't stall squaring things away, they prepared themselves quietly and in good time, deciding who should have the mare, who the foal. . . . And they departed easily, as if they were just moving into a new house.

ALEXANDER SOLZHENITSYN (1918–)

The Long Uphill Climb

It isn't for the moment you are struck that you need courage. But for the long uphill climb back to sanity and faith and security.

ANNE MORROW LINDBERGH (1906–2001)

from King Lear

ACT V, SCENE II

What, in ill thoughts again? Men must endure
Their going hence, even as their coming hither;
Ripeness is all.

WILLIAM SHAKESPEARE (1564–1616)

from Dombey and Son

And can it be that in a world so full and busy, the loss of one weak creature makes a void in any heart, so wide and deep that nothing but the width and depth of vast eternity can fill it up!

CHARLES DICKENS (1812–70)

One Person

Sometimes when one person is missing, the whole world seems depopulated.

ALPHONSE DE LAMARTINE (1790–1869)

MISSING

She Is Gone

Words from the poem that prefaced the Order of Service at Westminster Abbey for the Queen Mother's funeral.

You can shed tears that she is gone
or you can smile because she has lived.

You can close your eyes and pray that she'll come back
or you can open your eyes and see all she's left.

Your heart can be empty because you can't see her
or you can be full of the love you shared.

You can turn your back on tomorrow and live yesterday
or you can be happy for tomorrow because of yesterday.

You can remember her and only that she's gone
or you can cherish her memory and let it live on.

You can cry and close your mind, be empty and turn your
    back
or you can do what she'd want: smile, open your eyes, love
    and go on.

ANONYMOUS

The Walk

You did not walk with me
Of late to the hill-top tree
   By the gated ways,
   As in earlier days;
   You were weak and lame,
   So you never came,
And I went alone, and I did not mind,
Not thinking of you as left behind.

I walked up there to-day
Just in the former way;
   Surveyed around
   The familiar ground
   By myself again;
   What difference, then?
Only that underlying sense
Of the look of a room on returning thence.

THOMAS HARDY (1840–1928)

The Widower

For a season there must be pain –
For a little, little space
I shall lose the sight of her face,
Take back the old life again
While She is at rest in her place.

For a season this pain must endure,
For a little, little while
I shall sigh more often than smile
Till Time shall work me a cure,
And the pitiful days beguile.

For that season we must be apart,
For a little length of years,
Till my life's last hour nears,
And, above the beat of my heart,
I hear Her voice in my ears.

But I shall not understand –
Being set on some later love,
Shall not know her for whom I strove,
Till she reach me forth her hand,
Saying, 'Who but I have the right?'
And out of a troubled night
Shall draw me safe to the land.

RUDYARD KIPLING (1865–1936)

from The Child in Time

... Traffic, steady drizzle, shoppers waiting patiently at the zebra crossing, it was a wonder that there could be so much movement, so much purpose, all the time. He himself had none at all. He knew he wasn't going. He felt the air leaving him slowly, without a sound, and his chest and spine shrink. Almost three years on and still stuck, still trapped in the dark, enfolded with his loss, shaped by it, lost to the ordinary currents of feeling that moved far above him and belonged exclusively to other people. He brought to mind the three-year-old, the springy touch of her, how she fitted herself so comfortably round his body, the solemn purity of her voice, the wet red and white of tongue and lips and teeth, the unconditional trust. It was getting harder to recall. She was fading, and all the time his useless love was swelling, encumbering and disfiguring him like a goitre. He thought, I want you. I want you back. I want you brought back now. I don't want anything else.

IAN McEWAN (1948–)

How It Is

Shall I say how it is in your clothes?
A month after your death I wear your blue jacket.
The dog at the center of my life recognizes
you've come to visit, he's ecstatic.
In the left pocket, a hole.
In the right, a parking ticket
delivered up last August on Bay State Road.
In my heart, a scatter like milkweed,
a flinging from the pods of the soul.
My skin presses your old outline.
It is hot and dry inside.

I think of the last day of your life,
old friend, how I would unwind it, paste
it together in a different collage,
back from the death car idling in the garage,
back up the stairs, your praying hands unlaced,
reassembling the bites of bread and tuna fish
into a ceremony of sandwich,
running the home movie backward to a space
we could be easy in, a kitchen place
with vodka and ice, our words like living meat.

Dear friend, you have excited crowds
with your example. They swell
like wine bags, straining at your seams.
I will be years gathering up our words,
fishing out letters, snapshots, stains,
leaning my ribs against this durable cloth
to put on the dumb blue blazer of your death.

MAXINE KUMIN (1925–)

Remembrance

Cold in the earth – and the deep snow piled above thee!
    Far, far removed, cold in the dreary grave!
Have I forgot, my Only Love, to love thee,
    Severing at last by Time's all-severing wave?

Now, when alone, do my thoughts no longer hover
    Over the mountains, on that northern shore;
Resting their wings where heath and fern-leaves cover
    That noble heart for ever, ever more?

Cold in the earth – and fifteen wild Decembers
    From those brown hills have melted into spring:
Faithful indeed is the spirit that remembers
    After such years of change and suffering!

Sweet Love of youth, forgive, if I forget thee
    While the World's tide is bearing me along:
Other desires and other hopes beset me,
    Hopes which obscure, but cannot do thee wrong.

No later light has lightened up my heaven,
    No other Star has ever shone for me:
All my life's bliss from thy dear life was given –
    All my life's bliss is in the grave with thee.

But, when the days of golden dreams had perished,
    And even Despair was powerless to destroy;
Then did I learn how existence could be cherished,
    Strengthened and fed without the aid of joy;

Then did I check the tears of useless passion –
    Weaned my young soul from yearning after thine;
Sternly denied its burning wish to hasten
    Down to that tomb already more than mine.

And even yet, I dare not let it languish,
  Dare not indulge in Memory's rapturous pain;
Once drinking deep of that divinest anguish,
  How could I seek the empty world again?

EMILY BRONTË (1818–48)

Time Does Not Bring Relief

Time does not bring relief; you all have lied
   Who told me time would ease me of my pain!
   I miss him in the weeping of the rain;
I want him at the shrinking of the tide;
The old snows melt from every mountain-side,
   And last year's leaves are smoke in every lane;
   But last year's bitter loving must remain
Heaped on my heart, and my old thoughts abide!
There are a hundred places where I fear
   To go, – so with his memory they brim.
And entering with relief some quiet place
Where never fell his foot or shone his face
I say, 'There is no memory of him here!'
   And so stand stricken, so remembering him.

EDNA ST VINCENT MILLAY (1892–1950)

I'm Here for a Short Visit Only

I'm here for a short visit only,
And I'd rather be loved than hated.
Eternity may be lonely
When my body's disintegrated;
And that which is loosely termed my soul
Goes whizzing off through the infinite
By means of some vague remote control.
I'd like to think I was missed a bit.

NOËL COWARD (1899–1973)

If I Should Go Before the Rest of You

If I should go before the rest of you,
Break not a flower nor inscribe a stone.
Nor when I'm gone speak in a Sunday voice,
But be the usual selves that I have known.
Weep if you must,
Parting is hell,
But life goes on,
So sing as well.

JOYCE GRENFELL (1910–79)

from The Letters

They that mean to make no use of friends, will be at little trouble to gain them; and to be without friendship, is to be without one of the first comforts of our present state. To have no assistance from other minds, in resolving doubts, in appeasing scruples, in balancing deliberations, is a very wretched destitution. There is no wisdom in useless and hopeless sorrow, but there is something in it so like virtue, that he who is wholly without it cannot be loved, nor . . . be thought worthy of esteem. The loss of such a friend as has been taken from us increases our need of one another, and ought to unite us more closely.

DR JOHNSON (1709–84)

Losing a Friend

When we lose a friend we die a little.

ANONYMOUS

The Heart

What the heart has once known, it shall never forget.

ANONYMOUS

Remembering

REMEMBERING

from Captain Corelli's Mandolin

FOR HER I EAT AUBERGINES

When loved ones die, you have to live on their behalf. See things as though with their eyes. Remember how they used to say things, and use those words oneself. Be thankful that you can do things that they cannot, and also feel the sadness of it. This is how I live without Pelagia's mother. I have no interest in flowers, but for her I will look at a rock-rose or a lily. For her I eat aubergines, because she loved them.

LOUIS DE BERNIÈRES (1954–)

No Funeral Gloom

No funeral gloom, my dears, when I am gone,
Corpse-gazing, tears, black raiment, graveyard grimness.
Think of me as withdrawn into the dimness,
Yours still, you mine.
Remember all the best of our past moments and forget
      the rest,
And so to where I wait come gently on.

ELLEN TERRY (1848–1928)

The Voice

Woman much missed, how you call to me, call to me,
Saying that now you are not as you were
When you had changed from the one who was all to me,
But as at first, when our day was fair.

Can it be you that I hear? Let me view you, then,
Standing as when I drew near to the town
Where you would wait for me: yes, as I knew you then,
Even to the original air-blue gown!

Or is it only the breeze, in its listlessness
Travelling across the wet mead to me here,
You being ever dissolved to wan wistlessness,
Heard no more again far or near?

   Thus I; faltering forward,
   Leaves around me falling,
Wind oozing thin through the thorn from norward,
   And the woman calling.

THOMAS HARDY (1840–1928)

from A Grief Observed

Something quite unexpected has happened. It came this morning early. For various reasons, not in themselves at all mysterious, my heart was lighter than it had been for many weeks. For one thing, I suppose I am recovering physically from a good deal of mere exhaustion. And I'd had a very tiring but very healthy twelve hours the day before, and a sounder night's sleep; and after ten days of low-hung grey skies and motionless warm dampness, the sun was shining and there was a light breeze. And suddenly at the very moment when, so far, I mourned H. least, I remembered her best. Indeed it was something (almost) better than memory; an instantaneous, unanswerable impression. To say it was like a meeting would be going too far. Yet there was that in it which tempts one to use those words. It was as if the lifting of the sorrow removed a barrier.

Why has no one told me these things? How easily I might have misjudged another man in the same situation. I might have said, 'He's got over it. He's forgotten his wife', when the truth was, 'He remembers her better *because* he has partly got over it.' . . .

Looking back, I see that only a very little time ago I was greatly concerned about my memory of H. and how false it might become. For some reason – the merciful good sense of God is the only one I can think of – I have stopped bothering about that. And the remarkable thing is that since I stopped bothering about it, she seems to meet me everywhere. *Meet* is far too strong a word. I don't mean anything remotely like an apparition or a voice. I don't mean even any strikingly emotional experience at any particular moment. Rather, a sort of unobtrusive but massive sense that she is, just as much as ever, a fact to be taken into account.

C. S. LEWIS (1898–1963)

Memory Does Not Pass Away

The mists rise over
The still pools at Asuka.
Memory does not
Pass away so easily.

AKAHITO
(active *c.*724–37)

So Many Different Lengths of Time

Cuanto vive el hombre por fin? Vive mil dias o uno solo?
Una semana o varios siglos? Por cuanto tiempo muere el hombre?
Que quiere decir 'para siempre'?
Preocupado per este asunto me dedique a aclarar las cosas.

— PABLO NERUDA

How long is a man's life, finally?
Is it a thousand days, or only one?
One week, or a few centuries?
How long does a man's death last?
And what do we mean when we say, 'gone forever'?

Adrift in such preoccupations, we seek clarification.
We can go to the philosophers
but they will grow tired of our questions.
We can go to the priests and the rabbis
but they might be too busy with administrations.

★ ★ ★

So, how long does a man live, finally?
And how much does he live while he lives?
We fret, and ask so many questions –
then when it comes to us
the answer is so simple.

A man lives for as long as we carry him inside us,
for as long as we carry the harvest of his dreams,
for as long as we ourselves live,
holding memories in common, a man lives.

His lover will carry his man's scent, his touch;
his children will carry the weight of his love.
One friend will carry his arguments,

another will hum his favourite tunes,
another will still share his terrors.

And the days will pass with baffled faces,
then the weeks, then the months,
then there will be a day when no question is asked,
and the knots of grief will loosen in the stomach,
and the puffed faces will calm.
And on that day he will not have ceased,
but will have ceased to be separated by death.
How long does a man live, finally?

A man lives so many different lengths of time.

BRIAN PATTEN (1946–)

Comparisons

To all light things
I compared her; to
a snowflake, a feather.

I remember she rested
at the dance on my
arm, as a bird

on its nest lest
the eggs break, lest
she lean too heavily

on our love. Snow
melts, feathers
are blown away;

I have let
her ashes down
in me like an anchor.

R. S. THOMAS
(1913–2000)

A Letter from the Caribbean

Breezeways in the tropics winnow the air,
Are ajar to its least breath
But hold back, in a feint of architecture,
The boisterous sun
Pouring down upon

The island like a cloudburst. They
Slant to loft air, they curve, they screen
The wind's wild gaiety
Which tosses palm
Branches about like a marshal's plumes.

Within this filtered, latticed
World, where spools of shadow
Form, lift and change,
The triumph of incoming air
Is that it is there,

Cooling and salving us. Louvres,
Trellises, vines – music also –
Shape the arboreal wind, make skeins
Of it, and a maze
To catch shade. The days

Are all variety, blowing;
Aswirl in a perpetual current
Of wind, shadow, sun,
I marvel at the capacity
Of memory

Which, in some deep pocket
Of my mind, preserves you whole –
As wind is wind, as the lion-taming
Sun is sun, you are, you stay:
Nothing is lost, nothing has blown away.

BARBARA HOWES (1914–96)

M–M–Memory

Scooping spilt, soft, broken oil
with a silver spoon
from a flagstone floor
into a clay bowl –

the dull scrape of the spoon
on the cool stone,
lukewarm drops in the bowl –

m–m–memory.

Kneel there,
words like fossils
trapped in the roof of the mouth,
forgotten, half-forgotten, half-
recalled, the tongue dreaming
it can trace their shape.

Names, ghosts, m–memory.

Through the high window of the hall
clouds obfuscate the sun
and you sit, exhaling grey smoke
into a purpling, religious light
trying to remember everything

perfectly
in time and space
where you cannot.

Those unstrung beads of oil
seem precious now, now
that the light has changed.

CAROL ANN DUFFY (1965–)

from Auld Lang Syne

Should auld acquaintance be forgot,
   And never brought to min'?
Should auld acquaintance be forgot,
   And auld lang syne?

For auld lang syne, my dear,
   For auld lang syne,
We'll tak' a cup o'kindness yet,
   For auld lang syne.

ROBERT BURNS (1759–96)

Remember

Remember me when I am gone away,
   Gone far away into the silent land;
   When you can no more hold me by the hand,
Nor I half turn to go yet turning stay.
Remember me when no more day by day
   You tell me of our future that you planned:
   Only remember me; you understand
It will be late to counsel then or pray.
Yet if you should forget me for a while
   And afterwards remember, do not grieve:
   For if the darkness and corruption leave
   A vestige of the thoughts that once I had,
Better by far you should forget and smile
   Than that you should remember and be sad.

CHRISTINA ROSSETTI (1830–94)

Afterwards

When the Present has latched its postern behind my
    tremulous stay,
  And the May month flaps its glad green leaves like wings,
Delicate-filmed as new-spun silk, will the neighbours say,
    'He was a man who used to notice such things'?

If it be in the dusk when, like an eyelid's soundless blink,
  The dewfall-hawk comes crossing the shades to alight
Upon the wind-warped upland thorn, a gazer may think,
    'To him this must have been a familiar sight.'

If I pass during some nocturnal blackness, mothy and warm,
  When the hedgehog travels furtively over the lawn,
One may say, 'He strove that such innocent creatures should
    come to no harm,
    But he could do little for them; and now he is gone.'

If, when hearing that I have been stilled at last, they stand at
    the door,
  Watching the full-starred heavens that winter sees,
Will this thought rise on those who will meet my face no
    more,
    'He was one who had an eye for such mysteries'?

And will any say when my bell of quittance is heard in the
    gloom,
  And a crossing breeze cuts a pause in its outrollings,
Till they rise again, as they were a new bell's boom,
    'He hears it not now, but used to notice such things'?

THOMAS HARDY (1840–1928)

In Broad Daylight I Dream of My Dead Wife

Who says that the dead do not think of us?
Whenever I travel, she goes with me.
She was uneasy when I was on a journey.
She always wanted to accompany me.
While I dream, everything is as it used to be.
When I wake up, I am stabbed with sorrow.
The living are often parted and never meet again.
The dead are together as pure souls.

MEI YAO CH'EN (1002–60)

Song

When I am dead, my dearest,
  Sing no sad songs for me;
Plant thou no roses at my head,
  Nor shady cypress tree:
Be the green grass above me
  With showers and dewdrops wet;
And if thou wilt, remember,
  And if thou wilt, forget.

I shall not see the shadow,
  I shall not feel the rain;
I shall not hear the nightingale
  Sing on, as if in pain;
And dreaming through the twilight
  That doth not rise nor set,
Haply I may remember,
  And haply may forget.

CHRISTINA ROSSETTI (1830–94)

from The Fallen

They shall grow not old, as we that are left grow old:
  Age shall not weary them, nor the years condemn.
At the going down of the sun and in the morning
  We will remember them.

LAURENCE BINYON (1869–1943)

from Remembrance of Things Past

It is often said that something may survive of a person after his death, if that person was an artist and put a little of himself into his work. It is perhaps in the same way that a sort of cutting taken from one person and grafted on to the heart of another continues to carry on its existence even when the person from whom it had been detached has perished.

MARCEL PROUST (1871–1922)

A Sense of Proportion

If we treat the dead as if they were wholly dead it shows want of affection; if we treat them as wholly alive it shows want of sense. Neither should be done.

CONFUCIUS (c.551–c.479 BC)

The Life of the Dead

The life of the dead consists in being present in the minds of the living.

CICERO (106–43 BC)

Not Forgotten

To die completely, a person must not only forget but be forgotten, and he who is not forgotten is not dead.

SAMUEL BUTLER (1835–1902)

THANKSGIVING

from Thanksgivings for the Body

O what praises are due unto Thee,
    Who hast made me
        A living inhabitant
            Of the great world.
        And the centre of it!
        A sphere of sense,
            And a mine of riches,
Which when bodies are dissected fly away.
    The spacious room
        Which Thou hast hidden in mine eye,
    The chambers for sounds
        Which Thou hast prepar'd in mine ear,
    The receptacles for smells
        Concealed in my nose;
    The feeling of my hands,
        The taste of my tongue.
    But above all, O Lord, the glory of speech,
whereby Thy servant is enabled with praise to
celebrate Thee.
                For
    All the beauties in Heaven and earth,
    The melody of sounds,
    The sweet odours
        Of Thy dwelling-place.
    The delectable pleasures that gratify my sense,
        That gratify the feeling of mankind.
    The light of history,
        Admitted by the ear.
    The light of Heaven,
        Brought in by the eye.
    The volubility and liberty
        Of my hands and members.
    Fitted by Thee for all operations;
        Which the fancy can imagine,

       Or soul desire:
From the framing of a needle's eye,
    To the building of a tower:
From the squaring of trees,
    To the polishing of kings' crowns.
For all the mysteries, engines, instruments,
wherewith the world is filled, which we are able
to frame and use to Thy glory.
For all the trades, variety of operations, cities,
temples, streets, bridges, mariner's compass,
admirable pictures, sculpture, writing, printing,
songs and music, wherewith the world is
beautified and adorned.

THOMAS TRAHERNE (1637–74)

from Lines Composed a Few Miles above Tintern Abbey, on Revisiting the Banks of the Wye During a Tour. July 13 1798

                 For I have learned
To look on nature, not as in the hour
Of thoughtless youth; but hearing oftentimes
The still, sad music of humanity,
Nor harsh nor grating, though of ample power
To chasten and subdue. And I have felt
A presence that disturbs me with the joy
Of elevated thoughts; a sense sublime
Of something far more deeply interfused,
Whose dwelling is the light of setting suns,
And the round ocean and the living air,
And the blue sky, and in the mind of man;
A motion and a spirit, that impels
All thinking things, all objects of all thought,
And rolls through all things.

WILLIAM WORDSWORTH (1770–1850)

Fern Hill

Now as I was young and easy under the apple boughs
Above the lilting house and happy as the grass was green,
   The night above the dingle starry,
     Time let me hail and climb
    Golden in the heydays of his eyes,
And honoured among wagons I was prince of the apple
        towns
And once below a time I lordly had the trees and leaves
    Trail with daisies and barley
   Down the rivers of the windfall light.

And as I was green and carefree, famous among the barns
About the happy yard and singing as the farm was home,
   In the sun that is young once only,
     Time let me play and be
    Golden in the mercy of his means,
And green and golden I was huntsman and herdsman, the
        calves
Sang to my horn, the foxes on the hills barked clear and cold,
    And the sabbath rang slowly
   In the pebbles of the holy streams.

All the sun long it was running, it was lovely, the hay
Fields high as the house, the tunes from the chimneys, it was
        air
   And playing, lovely and watery
    And fire green as grass.
    And nightly under the simple stars
As I rode to sleep the owls were bearing the farm away,
All the moon long I heard, blessed among stables, the night-
      jars
   Flying with the ricks, and the horses
    Flashing into the dark.

And then to awake, and the farm, like a wanderer white
With the dew, come back, the cock on his shoulder: it was all
    Shining, it was Adam and maiden.
        The sky gathered again
    And the sun grew round that very day,
So it must have been after the birth of the simple light
In the first, spinning place, the spellbound horses walking
        warm
    Out of the whinnying green stable
      On to the fields of praise.

And honoured among foxes and pheasants by the gay house
Under the new made clouds and happy as the heart was long,
    In the sun born over and over,
      I ran my heedless ways,
    My wishes raced through the house high hay
And nothing I cared, at my sky blue trades, that time allows
In all his tuneful turning so few and such morning songs
    Before the children green and golden
      Follow him out of grace,

Nothing I cared, in the lamb white days, that time would
      take me
Up to the swallow thronged loft by the shadow of my hand,
    In the moon that is always rising,
      Nor that riding to sleep
    I should hear him fly with the high fields
And wake to the farm forever fled from the childless land.
Oh as I was young and easy in the mercy of his means,
    Time held me green and dying
    Though I sang in my chains like the sea.

DYLAN THOMAS (1914–53)

A Song of Living

Because I have loved life, I shall have no sorrow to die.
I have sent up my gladness on wings, to be lost in the
blue of the sky.
I have run and leaped with the rain, I have taken the
wind to my breast.
My cheek like a drowsy child to the face of the earth I
have pressed.
Because I have loved life, I shall have no sorrow to die.
I have kissed young Love on the lips, I have heard his
song to the end.
I have struck my hand like a seal in the loyal hand of a
friend.
I have known the peace of heaven, the comfort of
work done well.
I have longed for death in the darkness and risen alive
out of hell.
Because I have loved life, I shall have no sorrow to die.
I give a share of my soul to the world where my
course is run.
I know that another shall finish the task I must leave
undone.
I know that no flower, no flint was in vain on the path
I trod.
As one looks on a face through a window, through life
I have looked on God.
Because I have loved life, I shall have no sorrow to die.

AMELIA JOSEPHINE BURR (1878–?)

The Soldier

If I should die, think only this of me:
    That there's some corner of a foreign field
That is for ever England. There shall be
    In that rich earth a richer dust concealed;
A dust whom England bore, shaped, made aware,
    Gave, once, her flowers to love, her ways to roam,
A body of England's, breathing English air,
    Washed by the rivers, blest by suns of home.

And think, this heart, all evil shed away,
    A pulse in the eternal mind, no less
        Gives somewhere back the thoughts by England given;
Her sights and sounds; dreams happy as her day;
    And laughter, learnt of friends; and gentleness,
        In hearts at peace, under an English heaven.

RUPERT BROOKE (1887–1915)

Pied Beauty

Glory be to God for dappled things –
    For skies of couple-colour as a brinded cow;
      For rose-moles all in stipple upon trout that swim;
Fresh-firecoal chestnut-falls; finches' wings;
    Landscape plotted and pieced–fold, fallow, and plough;
      And áll trádes, their gear and tackle and trim.

All things counter, original, spare, strange;
    Whatever is fickle, freckled (who knows how?)
      With swift, slow; sweet, sour; adazzle, dim;
He fathers-forth whose beauty is past change:
          Praise him.

GERARD MANLEY HOPKINS (1844–89)

Ecstasy

You do not need to leave – remain sitting and listen;
Be quiet and still, and the world will freely offer
itself to you to be unmasked;
it has no choice –
it will roll in ecstasy at your feet.

FRANZ KAFKA (1883–1924)

God's Grandeur

The world is charged with the grandeur of God.
  It will flame out, like shining from shook foil;
  It gathers to a greatness, like the ooze of oil
Crushed. Why do men then now not reck his rod?
Generations have trod, have trod, have trod;
  And all is seared with trade; bleared, smeared with toil;
  And wears man's smudge and shares man's smell: the soil
Is bare now, nor can foot feel, being shod.

And for all this, nature is never spent;
  There lives the dearest freshness deep down things;
And though the last lights off the black West went
  Oh, morning, at the brown brink eastward, springs –
Because the Holy Ghost over the bent
  World broods with warm breast and with ah! bright wings.

GERARD MANLEY HOPKINS (1844–89)

Praise Life

Men and boughs break;
Praise life while you walk and wake,
It is only lent

DAVID CAMPBELL (1915–79)

FACING ETERNITY

from The Essays

There is no place on earth where death cannot find us — even if we constantly twist our heads about in all directions as in a dubious and suspect land . . . If there were any way of sheltering from death's blows — I am not the man to recoil from it . . . But it is madness to think that you can succeed . . .

Men come and they go and they trot and they dance, and never a word about death. All well and good. Yet when death does come — to them, their wives, their children, their friends — catching them unawares and unprepared, then what storms of passion overwhelm them, what cries, what fury, what despair! . . .

To begin depriving death of its greatest advantage over us, let us adopt a way clean contrary to that common one; let us deprive death of its strangeness, let us frequent it, let us get used to it; let us have nothing more often in mind than death . . . We do not know where death awaits us: so let us wait for it everywhere. To practise death is to practise freedom. A man who has learned how to die has unlearned how to be a slave.

MICHEL DE MONTAIGNE (1533–92)

from Paradise Lost

　　　　　　　For who would lose,
Though full of pain, this intellectual being,
Those thoughts that wander through eternity,
To perish rather, swallow'd up and lost
In the wide womb of uncreated night
Devoid of sense and motion?

JOHN MILTON (1608–74)

from Adonais

AN ELEGY ON THE DEATH OF JOHN KEATS

The One remains, the many change and pass;
Heaven's light forever shines, Earth's shadows fly;
Life, like a dome of many-colour'd glass,
Stains the white radiance of Eternity,
Until Death tramples it to fragments.

PERCY BYSSHE SHELLEY (1792–1822)

Life Unbroken

Death is nothing at all.
I have only slipped away into the
next room.
I am I and you are you.
Whatever we were to each other,
that we are still . . .
Why should I be out of mind
because I am out of sight?
I am waiting for you for an interval.
Somewhere very near, just
around the corner.
All is well.

Life Unbroken (longer version)

Death is nothing at all. I have only slipped away into the next room. I am I and you are you. Whatever we were to each other that we are still. Call me by my old familiar name, speak of me in the easy way which you always used. Put no difference into your tone; wear no forced air of solemnity or sorrow. Laugh as we always laughed at the little jokes we enjoyed together. Play, smile, think of me, pray for me. Let my name be ever the household word that it always was. Let it be spoken without an effort, without the ghost of a shadow on it. Life means all that it ever meant. It is the same as it ever was; there is absolutely unbroken continuity. What is this death but a negligible accident? I am but waiting for you, for an interval, somewhere very near, just around the corner. All is well.

HENRY SCOTT HOLLAND (1847–1918)

Death Be Not Proud

Death be not proud, though some have called thee
Mighty and dreadful, for, thou art not so,
For, those, whom thou think'st, thou dost overthrow,
Die not, poor death, nor yet canst thou kill me.
From rest and sleep, which but thy pictures be,
Much pleasure, then from thee, much more must flow,
And soonest our best men with thee do go,
Rest of their bones, and soul's delivery.
Thou art slave to fate, chance, kings, and desperate men,
And dost with poison, war, and sickness dwell,
And poppy, or charms can make us sleep as well,
And better than thy stroke; why swell'st thou then?
One short sleep past, we wake eternally,
And death shall be no more, Death thou shalt die.

JOHN DONNE (1572–1631)

from The Prelude

Whether we be young or old,
Our destiny, our being's heart and home,
Is with infinitude, and only there;
With hope it is, hope that can never die
Effort, and expectation, and desire,
And something evermore about to be.

WILLIAM WORDSWORTH (1770–1850)

Eden Rock

They are waiting for me somewhere beyond Eden Rock:
My father, twenty-five, in the same suit
Of Genuine Irish Tweed, his terrier Jack
Still two years old and trembling at his feet.

My mother, twenty-three, in a sprigged dress
Drawn at the waist, ribbon in her straw hat,
Has spread the stiff white cloth over the grass.
Her hair, the colour of wheat, takes on the light.

She pours tea from a Thermos, the milk straight
From an old H.P. sauce bottle, a screw
Of paper for a cork; slowly sets out
The same three plates, the tin cups painted blue.

The sky whitens as if lit by three suns.
My mother shades her eyes and looks my way
Over the drifted stream. My father spins
A stone along the water. Leisurely,

They beckon to me from the other bank.
I hear them call, 'See where the stream-path is!
Crossing is not as hard as you might think.'

I had not thought that it would be like this.

CHARLES CAUSLEY (1917–2003)

'Goodnight, Willie Lee,
I'll See You in the Morning'

Looking down into my father's
dead face
for the last time
my mother said without
tears, without smiles
without regrets
but with *civility*
'Goodnight, Willie Lee, I'll see you
in the morning.'
And it was then I knew that the healing
of all our wounds
is forgiveness
that permits a promise
of our return
at the end.

ALICE WALKER (1944–)

And Death Shall Have No Dominion

And death shall have no dominion.
Dead men naked they shall be one
With the man in the wind and the west moon;
When their bones are picked clean and the clean bones gone.
They shall have stars at elbow and foot;
Though they go mad they shall be sane,
Though they sink through the sea they shall rise again;
Though lovers be lost love shall not;
And death shall have no dominion.

And death shall have no dominion.
Under the windings of the sea
They lying long shall not die windily;
Twisting on racks when sinews give way,
Strapped to a wheel, yet they shall not break;
Faith in their hands shall snap in two,
And the unicorn evils run them through;
Split all ends up they shan't crack;
And death shall have no dominion.

And death shall have no dominion.
No more may gulls cry at their ears
Or waves break loud on the seashores;
Where blew a flower may a flower no more
Lift its head to the blows of the rain;
Though they be made and dead as nails,
Heads of the characters hammer through daisies;
Break in the sun till the sun breaks down,
And death shall have no dominion.

DYLAN THOMAS (1914–53)

No Coward Soul

No coward soul is mine,
No trembler in the world's storm-troubled sphere:
I see Heaven's glories shine,
And Faith shines equal, arming me from fear.

O God within my breast,
Almighty, ever-present Deity!
Life – that in me has rest,
As I – undying Life – have power in thee!

Vain are the thousand creeds
That move men's hearts: unutterably vain;
Worthless as withered weeds,
Or idlest froth amid the boundless main,

To waken doubt in one
Holding so fast by thine infinity;
So surely anchored on
The steadfast rock of immortality.

With wide-embracing love
Thy spirit animates eternal years,
Pervades and broods above,
Changes, sustains, dissolves, creates, and rears.

Though earth and man were gone,
And suns and universes ceased to be,
And thou were left alone,
Every existence would exist in thee.

There is not room for Death,
Nor atom that his might could render void:
Thou – thou art Being and Breath,
And what thou art may never be destroyed.

EMILY BRONTË (1818–48)

from The Apology of Socrates

The fear of death is the pretence of wisdom, and not real wisdom, being a pretence of knowing the unknown; and no one knows whether death, which men in their fear apprehend to be the greatest evil, may not be the greatest good. Is not this ignorance of a disgraceful sort, the ignorance which is the conceit that man knows what he does not know? . . .

[T]here is great reason to hope that death is a good; for one of two things – either death is a state of nothingness and utter unconsciousness, or, as men say, there is a change and migration of the soul from this world to another. Now if you suppose that there is no consciousness, but a sleep like the sleep of him who is undisturbed even by dreams, death will be an unspeakable gain . . . Now if death be of such a nature, I say that to die is gain; for eternity is then only a single night. But if death is the journey to another place, and there, as men say, all the dead abide, what good, O my friends and judges, can be greater than this? . . . What would not a man give if he might converse with Orpheus and . . . Hesiod and Homer? Nay, if this be true, let me die again and again . . . I shall then be able to continue my search into true and false knowledge; as in this world, so also in the next and I shall find out who is wise, and who pretends to be wise, and is not. What would not a man give, O judges, to be able to examine the leader of the great Trojan expedition; or Odysseus or Sisyphus, or numberless others, men and women too! What infinite delight would there be in conversing with them and asking them questions! In another world they do not put a man to death for asking questions: assuredly not. For besides being happier than we are, they will be immortal, if what is said is true.

Wherefore, O judges, be of good cheer about death, and know of a certainty, that no evil can happen to a good man, either in life or after death.

PLATO (c.429–347 BC)

Everything Passes and Vanishes

Everything passes and vanishes;
Everything leaves its trace;
And often you see in a footstep
What you could not see in a face.

WILLIAM ALLINGHAM (1924–89)

Heredity

I am the family face;
Flesh perishes, I live on,
Projecting trait and trace
Through time to times anon,
And leaping from place to place
Over oblivion.

The years-heired feature that can
In curve and voice and eye
Despise the human span
Of durance – that is I;
The eternal thing in man,
That heeds no call to die.

THOMAS HARDY (1840–1928)

from Letter to Menoeceus

So death, the most terrifying of ills, is nothing to us, since so long as we exist, death is not with us; but when death comes, then we do not exist. It does not then concern either the living or the dead, since for the former it is not, and the latter are no more.

Epicurus (341–270 bc)

from The Night

There is in God (some say)
A deep, but dazzling darkness; As men here
Say it is late and dusky, because they
    See not all clear;
  O for that night! where I in him
Might live invisible and dim.

HENRY VAUGHAN (*c.*1621–95)

High Flight (An Airman's Ecstasy)

Oh, I have slipped the surly bonds of earth
And danced the skies on laughter-silvered wings;
Sunward I've climbed and joined the tumbling mirth
Of sun-split clouds – and done a hundred things
You have not dreamed of; wheeled and soared and swung
High in the sun-lit silence. Hovering there
I've chased the shouting wind along, and flung
My eager craft through footless halls of air;
Up, up the long, delirious, burning blue
I've topped the wind-swept heights with easy grace,
Where never lark nor even eagle flew;
And while, with silent lifting mind I've trod
The high untrespassed sanctity of space,
Put out my hand, and touched the face of God.

JOHN GILLESPIE MAGEE (1922–41)

The Long Habit of Living

The long habit of living indisposeth us to dying.

THOMAS BROWNE (1605–82)

from Meditations

Death: a release from impressions of sense, from twitchings of appetite, from excursions of thought, and from service to the flesh.

MARCUS AURELIUS (AD 121–180)

from A Confession

The essence of every faith consists in its giving life a meaning which death cannot destroy.

LEO TOLSTOY (1828–1910)

Old Irish Toast

May you have food and raiment,
A soft pillow for your head,
May you be forty years in heaven
Before the devil knows you're dead.

ANONYMOUS

SEEING THE
PATTERN

To Every Thing There Is a Season

To every thing there is a season, and a time to every purpose under the heaven: a time to be born, and a time to die; a time to plant, and a time to pluck up that which is planted; a time to kill, and a time to heal; a time to break down, and a time to build up; a time to weep, and a time to laugh; a time to mourn, and a time to dance; a time to cast away stones, and a time to gather stones together; a time to embrace, and a time to refrain from embracing; a time to get, and a time to lose; a time to keep, and a time to cast away; a time to rend, and a time to sew; a time to keep silence, and a time to speak; a time to love, and a time to hate; a time of war, and a time of peace.

ECCLESIASTES 3: 1–8

from Burnt Norton, *Four Quartets*

Time present and time past
Are both perhaps present in time future,
And time future contained in time past.
If all time is eternally present
All time is unredeemable.
What might have been is an abstraction
Remaining a perpetual possibility
Only in a world of speculation.
What might have been and what has been
Point to one end, which is always present.
Footfalls echo in the memory
Down the passage which we did not take
Towards the door we never opened
Into the rose-garden.

T. S. ELIOT (1888–1965)

from The Tempest

Full fathom five thy father lies;
   Of his bones are coral made;
Those are pearls that were his eyes;
   Nothing of him that doth fade,
But doth suffer a sea-change
Into something rich and strange.
Sea-nymphs hourly ring his knell:
     Ding-dong.
   Hark! now I hear them,
     Ding-dong, bell.

WILLIAM SHAKESPEARE (1564–1616)

from The Prophet

ON DEATH

You would know the secret of death.

But how shall you find it unless you seek it in the heart of life?

The owl whose night-bound eyes are blind unto the day cannot unveil the mystery of light.

If you would indeed behold the spirit of death, open your heart wide unto the body of life.

For life and death are one, even as the river and the sea are one.

In the depth of your hopes and desires lies your silent knowledge of the beyond;

And like seeds dreaming beneath the snow your heart dreams of spring.

Trust the dreams, for in them is hidden the gate to eternity.

Your fear of death is but the trembling of the shepherd when he stands before the king whose hand is to be laid upon him in honour.

Is the shepherd not joyful beneath his trembling, that he shall wear the mark of the king?

Yet is he not more mindful of his trembling?

For what is it to die but to stand naked in the wind and to melt into the sun?

And what is it to cease breathing but to free the breath from its restless tides, that it may rise and expand and seek God unencumbered?

Only when you drink from the river of silence shall you indeed sing.

And when you have reached the mountain top, then you shall begin to climb.

And when the earth shall claim your limbs, then shall you truly dance.

KAHLIL GIBRAN (1883–1931)

from Esarhaddon, King of Assyria

'Do you understand,' the old man continued, 'that Lailie is you, that the warriors you put to death also were you? And that not only the warriors, but the animals you hunted and slew and afterwards devoured at your feasts, they were you. You thought life dwelt in you alone, but I have drawn aside the veil of delusion, and you have seen that in doing evil to others you have done it to yourself as well. Life is one in everything, and within yourself you manifest but a portion of this one life. And only in that portion that is within you can you make life better or worse, magnify or diminish it. You can make life better within yourself only by destroying the barriers that divide your life from that of others, and by regarding others as yourself and loving them. To destroy the life that dwells in others is not within your power. The life that was in those you have slain has not been destroyed: it has merely vanished from before your eyes. You thought to prolong your own life and to shorten the lives of others, but you cannot do this, for life there is neither time nor space. The life of a moment and the life of thousands of years, your life and the lives of all creatures seen and unseen, is one. To destroy life, even to alter it, is impossible, for life alone exists. All else only seems to be.'

Leo Tolstoy (1828–1910)

from The Prophet

ON PAIN

Your pain is the breaking of the shell that encloses your understanding.

Even as the stone of the fruit must break, that its heart may stand in the sun, so must you know pain.

And could you keep your heart in wonder at the daily miracles of your life, your pain would not seem less wondrous than your joy;

And you would accept the seasons of your heart, even as you have always accepted the seasons that pass over your fields.

And you would watch with serenity through the winters of your grief.

KAHLIL GIBRAN (1883–1931)

from The Bhagavad Gita

CHAPTER 2
LIFE AND DEATH SHALL PASS AWAY

Thy tears are for those beyond tears; and are thy words words of wisdom? The wise grieve not for those who live; and they grieve not for those who die – for life and death shall pass away.

Because we all have been for all time: I, and thou, and those kings of men. And we all shall be for all time, we all for ever and ever.

As the Spirit of our mortal body wanders on in childhood, and youth and old age, the Spirit wanders on to a new body: of this the sage has no doubts.

From the world of the senses, Arjuna, comes heat and comes cold, and pleasure and pain. They come and they go: they are transient. Arise above them, strong soul.

The man whom these cannot move, whose soul is one, beyond pleasure and pain, is worthy of life in Eternity.

The unreal never is: the Real never is not. This truth indeed has been seen by those who can see the true.

Interwoven in his creation, the Spirit is beyond destruction. No one can bring to an end the Spirit which is everlasting.

For beyond time he dwells in these bodies, though these bodies have an end in their time; but he remains immeasurable, immortal . . .

He is never born, and he never dies. He is in Eternity: he is for evermore. Never-born and eternal, beyond times gone or to come, he does not die when the body dies . . .

As a man leaves an old garment and puts on one that is new, the Spirit leaves his mortal body and then puts on one that is new.

Weapons cannot hurt the Spirit and fire can never burn him. Untouched is he by drenching waters, untouched is he by parching winds.

Beyond the power of sword and fire, beyond the power of waters and winds, the Spirit is everlasting, omnipresent, never-changing, never-moving, ever One.

Invisible is he to mortal eyes, beyond thought and beyond change. Know that he is, and cease from sorrow.

But if he were born again and again, and again and again he were to die, even then, victorious man, cease thou from sorrow.

ANONYMOUS

from Little Gidding, *Four Quartets*

We shall not cease from exploration
And the end of all our exploring
Will be to arrive where we started
And know the place for the first time.
Through the unknown, remembered gate
When the last of earth left to discover
Is that which was the beginning;
At the source of the longest river
The voice of the hidden waterfall
And the children in the apple-tree
Not known, because not looked for
But heard, half-heard, in the stillness
Between two waves of the sea.
Quick now, here, now, always –
A condition of complete simplicity
(Costing not less than everything)
And all shall be well and
All manner of thing shall be well
When the tongues of flames are in-folded
Into the crowned knot of fire
And the fire and the rose are one.

T. S. ELIOT (1888–1965)

from The Bhagavad Gita

CHAPTER 18

When one sees Eternity in things that pass away and Infinity in finite things, then one has pure knowledge.

But if one merely sees the diversity of things, with their diversions and limitations, then one has impure knowledge.

And if one selfishly sees a thing as if it were everything, independent of the ONE and the many, then one is in the darkness of ignorance.

ANONYMOUS

Everything Exists

For everything exists and not
one sigh nor smile nor tear,
one hair nor particle of
dust, not one can pass away.

WILLIAM BLAKE (1757–1827)

from The Taittiriya Upanished

And then he saw that Brahman is joy: for from joy all beings have come, by joy they all live, and unto joy they all return.

ANONYMOUS

Sanskrit Proverb, Look to This Day

Look to this day! For it is life, the very life of life. For yesterday is but a dream. And tomorrow is only a vision. But today well lived makes every yesterday a dream of happiness. And tomorrow a vision of hope. Look well, therefore, to this day!

ANONYMOUS

Inspiration

Praise of a Man

He went through a company like a lamplighter –
see the dull minds, one after another,
begin to glow, to shed
a beneficent light.

He went through a company like
a knifegrinder – see the dull minds
scattering sparks of themselves,
becoming razory, becoming useful.

He went through a company
as himself. But now he's one
of the multitudinous company of the dead
where are no individuals.

The beneficent lights dim
but don't vanish. The razory edges
dull, but still cut. He's gone: but you can see
his tracks still, in the snow of the world.

NORMAN MACCAIG (1910–96)

Epitaph on a Friend

An honest man here lies at rest,
The friend of man, the friend of truth,
The friend of age, and guide of youth:
Few hearts like his, with virtue warm'd,
Few heads with knowledge so inform'd;
If there's another world, he lives in bliss;
If there is none, he made the best of this.

ROBERT BURNS (1759–96)

The Good

The good are vulnerable
As any bird in flight,
They do not think of safety,
Are blind to possible extinction
And when most vulnerable
Are most themselves.
The good are real as the sun,
Are best perceived through clouds
Of casual corruption
That cannot kill the luminous sufficiency
That shines on city, sea and wilderness,
Fastidiously revealing
One man to another,
Who yet will not accept
Responsibilities of light.
The good incline to praise,
To have the knack of seeing that
The best is not destroyed
Although forever threatened.
The good go naked in all weathers,
And by their nakedness rebuke
The small protective sanities
That hide men from themselves.
The good are difficult to see
Though open, rare, destructible;
Always, they retain a kind of youth,
The vulnerable grace
Of any bird in flight,
Content to be itself,
Accomplished master and potential victim,
Accepting what the earth or sky intends.
I think that I know one or two
Among my friends.

BRENDAN KENNELLY (1936–)

Not, How Did He Die, but How Did He Live?

Not, how did he die, but how did he live?
Not, what did he gain, but what did he give?
These are the units to measure the worth
Of a man as a man, regardless of birth.
Not what was his church, nor what was his creed?
But had he befriended those really in need?
Was he ever ready, with word of good cheer,
To bring back a smile, to banish a tear?
Not what did the sketch in the newspaper say,
But how many were sorry when he passed away?

ANONYMOUS

Death Can Show Us the Way

Death can show us the way, for when we know and understand completely that our time on this earth is limited, and that we have no way of knowing when it will be over, then we must live each day as if it were the only one we had.

ELIZABETH KÜBLER-ROSS (1926–)

For Whom the Bell Tolls

All *mankinde* is of one *Author*, and is one *volume*; when one Man dies, one *Chapter* is not *torne* out of the *booke*, but *translated* into a better *language*; and every *Chapter* must be so *translated*; God emploies several *translators*; some peeces are translated by *age*, some by *sicknesse*, some by *warre*, some by *justice*; but *Gods* hand is in every *translation*; and his hand shall bind up all our scattered leaves againe, for that *Librarie* where every *booke* shall lie open to one another: As therefore the *Bell* that rings to a *Sermon*, calls not upon the *Preacher* onely, but upon the *Congregation* to come; so this *Bell* calls us all: but how much more mee, who am brought so neere the *doore* by this *sicknesse* . . .

The *Bell* doth toll for him that *thinkes* it doth; and though it *intermit* againe, yet from that *minute*, that that occasion wrought upon him, hee is united to *God*. Who casts not up his *Eye* to the *Sunne* when it rises? but who takes off his *Eye* from a *Comet* when that breakes out? Who bends not his *eare* to any *bell*, which upon any occasion rings? but who can remove it from that *bell*, which is passing a *peece of himselfe* out of this *world*? No man is an *Iland*, intire of it selfe; every man is a peece of the *Continent*, a part of the *maine*; if a *Clod* bee washed away by the *Sea*, *Europe* is the lesse, as well as if a *Promontorie* were, as well as if a *Mannor* of thy *friends* or of *thine owne* were; any mans *death* diminishes *me*, because I am involved in *Mankinde*; And therefore never send to know for whom the *bell* tolls; It tolls for *thee*.

JOHN DONNE (1572–1631)

Desiderata

GO PLACIDLY
AMID THE NOISE AND THE HASTE
AND REMEMBER WHAT PEACE
THERE MAY BE IN SILENCE

As far as possible without surrender be on good terms with all persons. Speak your truth quietly and listen to others, even the dull and ignorant; they too have their story. Avoid loud and aggressive persons, they are vexatious to the spirit. If you compare yourself to others, you may become vain and bitter, for always there will be greater and lesser persons than yourself.

Enjoy your achievements as well as your plans. Keep interested in your career however humble; it is a real possession in the changing fortunes of time. Exercise caution in your business affairs for the world is full of trickery. But let this not blind you to what virtue there is: many persons strive for high ideals, and everywhere life is full of heroism. Be yourself, especially do not feign affection. Neither be cynical about love; for in the face of all aridity and disenchantment it is as perennial as the grass. Take kindly the counsel of the years, gracefully surrendering the things of youth.

Nurture the strength of spirit to shield you in sudden misfortune. But do not distress yourself with imaginings. Many fears are born of fatigue and loneliness. Beyond a wholesome discipline, be gentle with yourself. You are a child of the universe, no less than the trees and the stars: you have a right to be here. And whether or not it is clear to you no doubt the universe is unfolding as it should.

Therefore be at peace with God, whatever you conceive Him to be; and whatever your labours and aspirations, in the noisy confusion of life, keep peace with your soul. With all its sham, drudgery and broken dreams, it is still a beautiful world.

Be cheerful. Strive to be happy.

MAX EHRMANN (1872-1945)

from The Idler, December 1759

What have ye done?

The fatal question has disturbed the quiet of many minds. He that in the latter part of his life too strictly enquires what he has done, can very seldom receive from his own heart such an account as will give him satisfaction. However, every man is obliged by the supreme master of the universe to improve all the opportunities of good which are afforded him, and to keep in continual activity such activities as are bestowed upon him. But he has no reason to repine though his abilities are small and his opportunities few. He that has improved the virtue or advanced the happiness of one fellow creature, he that has ascertained a simple moral proposition, or added one useful experiment to natural knowledge, may be contented with his own performance, and, with respect to mortals like himself, may demand, like Augustus, to be dismissed at his departure with applause.

DR JOHNSON (1709–84)

People

No people are uninteresting,
Their fate is like the chronicle of planets.

Nothing in them is not particular,
And planet is dissimilar from planet.

And if a man lived in obscurity
Making his friends in that obscurity,
Obscurity is not uninteresting.

To each his world is private,
And in that world one excellent minute,
And in that world one tragic minute,
These are private.

YEVGENY YEVTUSHENKO (1933–)

from Ulysses

I cannot rest from travel: I will drink
Life to the lees: all times I have enjoyed
Greatly, have suffer'd greatly, both with those
That loved me, and alone; on shore, and when
Thro' scuddying drifts the rainy Hyades
Vext the dim sea: I am become a name:
For always roaming with a hungry heart
Much have I seen and known; cities of men
And manners, climates, councils, governments,
Myself not least, but honour'd of them all;
And drunk delight of battle with my peers,
Far on the ringing plains of windy Troy.
I am a part of all that I have met;
Yet all experience is an arch wherethro'
Gleams that untravell'd world, whose margin fades
For ever and for ever when I move.
How dull it is to pause, to make an end,
To rust unburnish'd, not to shine in use!
As tho' to breathe were life. Life piled on life
Were all too little . . .
The lights begin to twinkle from the rocks:
The long day wanes: the slow moon climbs: the deep
Moans round with many voices. Come, my friends,
'Tis not too late to seek a newer world.
Push off, and sitting well in order smite
The sounding furrows; for my purpose holds
To sail beyond the sunset . . .
Tho' much is taken, much abides; and tho'
We are not now that strength which in old days
Moved earth and heaven; that which we are, we are;
One equal temper of heroic hearts,
Made weak by time and fate, but strong in will
To strive, to seek, to find, and not to yield.

ALFRED, LORD TENNYSON (1809–92)

I Think Continually of Those
Who Were Truly Great

I think continually of those who were truly great.
Who, from the womb, remembered the soul's history
Through corridors of light where the hours are suns
Endless and singing. Whose lovely ambition
Was that their lips, still touched with fire,
Should tell of the Spirit clothed from head to foot in song.
And who hoarded from the Spring branches
The desires falling across their bodies like blossoms.

What is precious, is never to forget
The delight of the blood drawn from ageless springs
Breaking through rocks in worlds before our earth;
Never to deny its pleasure in the morning simple light
Nor its grave evening demand for love.
Never to allow gradually the traffic to smother
With noise and fog, the flowering of the spirit.

Near the snow, near the sun, in the highest fields,
See how these names are fêted by the waving grass,
And by the streamers of white cloud,
And whispers of wind in the listening sky.
The names of those who in their lives fought for life,
Who wore at their hearts the fire's centre.
Born of the sun, they travelled a short while towards the sun,
And left the vivid air signed with their honour.

STEPHEN SPENDER (1909–95)

Decide How You're Going to Live

You don't get to choose how you're going to die, or when. You can only decide how you're going to live. Now.

JOAN BAEZ (1941–)

Part of a Long Story

The older I get, the more I habitually think of my own life as a relatively short episode in a long story of which it is a part.

A. S. BYATT (1936–)

The Act of Dying of No Importance

It matters not how a man dies, but how he lives. The act of dying is of no importance, it lasts so short a time.

DR JOHNSON (1709–84)

I Shall Not Pass This Way Again

I expect to pass through life but once. If, therefore, there be any kindness I can show, or any good thing I can do to any fellow being, let me do it now, for I shall not pass this way again.

WILLIAM PENN (1644–1718)

from An Elegy on the Death of John Donne

... the flame
Of thy brave Soule, that shot such heat and light
As burnt our earth, and made our darkness bright.

THOMAS CAREW (*c.* 1595–*c.* 1639)

Let Us Be Kinder

Spoken on his deathbed

Let us be kinder to one another.

ALDOUS HUXLEY (1894–1963)

LOVE'S POWER

Old Friends

Those that have loved longest love best. A sudden blaze of kindness may by a single blast of coldness be extinguished, but that fondness which length of time has connected with many circumstances and occasions, though it may for a while be suppressed by disgust or resentment, with or without a cause, is hourly revived by accidental recollection. To those who have lived long together, every thing heard, and every thing seen recalls some pleasure communicated, or some benefit conferred, some petty quarrel, or some slight endearment. Esteem of great powers, or amiable qualities newly discovered, may embroider a day or a week, but a friendship of many years is interwoven with the texture of life. A friend may be often found and lost; but an *old friend* never can be found, and nature has provided that he cannot easily be lost.

DR JOHNSON (1709–84)

For Katrina's Sun Dial

(Read at Princess Diana's funeral by her sister)

Time is too slow for those who wait,
Too swift for those who fear,
Too long for those who grieve,
Too short for those who rejoice,
But for those who love, time is
Eternity.

HENRY VAN DYKE (1852–1933)

Only Love and then Oblivion

A San Francisco husband slept through his wife's call from the World Trade Center. The tower was burning all around her, and she was speaking on her mobile phone. She left her last message to him on the answering machine. A TV station played it to us, while it showed the husband standing there listening. Somehow, he was able to bear hearing it again. We heard her tell him through her sobbing that there was no escape for her. The building was on fire and there was no way down the stairs. She was calling to say goodbye. There was really only one thing for her to say, those three words that all the terrible art, the worst pop songs and movies, the most seductive lies, can somehow never cheapen. I love you.

She said it over and again before the line went dead. And that is what they were all saying down their phones, from the hijacked planes and the burning towers. There is only love, and then oblivion. Love was all they had to set against the hatred of their murderers . . .

The hijackers used fanatical certainty, misplaced religious faith, and dehumanising hatred to purge themselves of the human instinct for empathy. Among their crimes was a failure of the imagination. As for their victims in the planes and in the towers, in their terror they would not have felt it at the time, but those snatched and anguished assertions of love were their defiance.

IAN MCEWAN (1948-)

An Arundel Tomb

Side by side, their faces blurred,
The earl and countess lie in stone,
Their proper habits vaguely shown
As jointed armour, stiffened pleat,
And that faint hint of the absurd –
The little dogs under their feet.

Such plainness of the pre-baroque
Hardly involves the eye, until
It meets his left-hand gauntlet, still
Clasped empty in the other; and
One sees, with a sharp tender shock
His hand withdrawn, holding her hand.

They would not think to lie so long.
Such faithfulness in effigy
Was just a detail friends would see:
A sculptor's sweet commissioned grace
Thrown off in helping to prolong
The Latin names around the base.

They would not guess how early in
Their supine stationary voyage
The air would change to soundless damage,
Turn the old tenantry away;
How soon succeeding eyes begin
To look, not read. Rigidly they

Persisted, linked, through lengths and breadths
Of time. Snow fell, undated. Light
Each summer thronged the glass. A bright
Litter of birdcalls strewed the same
Bone-riddled ground. And up the paths
The endless altered people came,

Washing at their identity.
Now, helpless in the hollow of
An unarmorial age, a trough
Of smoke in slow suspended skeins
Above their scrap of history,
Only an attitude remains:

Time has transfigured them into
Untruth. The stone fidelity
They hardly meant has come to be
Their final blazon, and to prove
Our almost-instinct almost true:
What will survive of us is love.

PHILIP LARKIN (1922–85)

from Sonnets from the Portuguese

XLIII

How do I love thee? Let me count the ways.
I love thee to the depth and breadth and height
My soul can reach, when feeling out of sight
For the ends of Being and ideal Grace.
I love thee to the level of everyday's
Most quiet need, by sun and candlelight.
I love thee freely, as men strive for Right;
I love thee purely, as they turn from Praise.
I love thee with the passion put to use
In my old griefs, and with my childhood's faith.
I love thee with a love I seemed to lose
With my lost saints, – I love thee with the breath,
Smiles, tears, of all my life! – and, if God choose,
I shall but love thee better after death.

ELIZABETH BARRETT BROWNING (1806–61)

Through a Glass Darkly

I CORINTHIANS 13

Though I speak with the tongues of men and of angels, and have not love, I am become as sounding brass, or a tinkling cymbal. And though I have the gift of prophecy, and understand all mysteries and all knowledge; and though I have all faith, so that I could remove mountains, and have not love, I am nothing. And though I bestow all my goods to feed the poor, and though I give my body to be burned, and have not love, it profiteth me nothing. Love suffereth long, and is kind; love envieth not; love vaunteth not itself, is not puffed up, doth not behave itself unseemly, seeketh not her own, is not easily provoked, thinketh no evil; rejoiceth not in iniquity, but rejoiceth in the truth; beareth all things, believeth all things, hopeth all things, endureth all things. Love never faileth: but whether there be prophecies, they shall fail; whether there be tongues, they shall cease; whether there be knowledge, it shall vanish away. For we know in part, and we prophesy in part. But when that which is perfect is come, then that which is in part shall be done away. When I was a child, I spake as a child, I understood as a child, I thought as a child: but when I became a man, I put away childish things. For now we see through a glass, darkly; but then face to face: now I know in part; but then shall I know even as also I am known. And now abideth faith, hope, love, these three; but the greatest of these is love.

Love Is Strong as Death

SONG OF SONGS 8: 6–7

For love is strong as death,
passion cruel as the grave;
    it blazes up like blazing fire,
    fiercer than any flame.
Many waters cannot quench love,
    no flood can sweep it away;
if a man were to offer for love
    the whole wealth of his house,
    it would be utterly scorned.

Code Poem for the French Resistance

The life that I have is all that I have,
And the life that I have is yours.
The love that I have of the life that I have
Is yours and yours and yours.

A sleep I shall have,
A rest I shall have,
Yet death will be but a pause,
For the peace of my years in the long green grass
Will be yours and yours and yours.

LEO MARKS (1920–2001)

Sonnet XXV

Let those who are in favour with their stars
Of public honour and proud titles boast,
Whilst I, whom fortune of such triumph bars
Unlook'd for joy in that I honour most;
Great princes' favourites their fair leaves spread
But as the marigold at the sun's eye,
And in themselves their pride lies buried,
For at a frown they in their glory die.
The painful warrior famoused for fight,
After a thousand victories once foil'd,
Is from the book of honour razed quite,
And all the rest forgot for which he toiled:
   Then happy I, that love and am beloved
   Where I may not remove nor be removed.

WILLIAM SHAKESPEARE (1564–1616)

To Joshua

All his beauty, wit and grace
Lie forever in one place.
He who sang and sprang and moved
Now, in death, is only loved.

ALICE THOMAS ELLIS (1932–)

The Bidding

The Queen Mother's Funeral, 9 April 2002

Love is immortal, and death is only an horizon, and an horizon is
nothing save the limit of our sight.

ROSSITER W. RAYMOND (1840–1918)

from Romeo and Juliet

ACT III SCENE II

. . . when he shall die,
Take him and cut him out in little stars,
And he will make the face of heaven so fine
That all the world will be in love with night
And pay no worship to the garish sun.

WILLIAM SHAKESPEARE (1564–1616)

FINDING PEACE

Do Not Stand at My Grave and Weep

Do not stand at my grave and weep;
I am not there. I do not sleep.
I am a thousand winds that blow.
I am the diamond glints on snow.
I am the sunlight on ripened grain.
I am the gentle autumn rain.
When you awaken in the morning's hush
I am the swift uplifting rush
Of quiet birds in circled flight.
I am the soft stars that shine at night.
Do not stand at my grave and cry;
I am not there. I did not die.

ANONYMOUS

The Lake Isle of Innisfree

I will arise and go now, and go to Innisfree,
And a small cabin build there, of clay and wattles made:
Nine bean-rows will I have there, a hive for the honey-bee,
And live alone in the bee-loud glade.

And I shall have some peace there, for peace comes
    dropping slow,
Dropping from the veils of the morning to where the
    cricket sings;
There midnight's all a glimmer, and noon a purple glow,
And evening full of the linnet's wings.

I will arise and go now, for always night and day
I hear lake water lapping with low sounds by the shore;
While I stand on the roadway, or on the pavements grey,
I hear it in the deep heart's core.

W. B. YEATS (1865–1939)

from The Last Hiding Places of Snow

Every so often, when I look
at the dark sky, I know she remains
among the old endless blue lightedness
· of stars; or finding myself out in a field
in November, when a strange
starry perhaps first snowfall blows
down across the darkening air, lightly,
I know she is there, where snow
falls flakes down fragile softly
falling until I can't see the world
any longer, only its stilled shapes.

GALWAY KINNELL (1927–)

from Adonais

Peace, peace! he is not dead, he doth not sleep,
He hath awaken'd from the dream of life;
'Tis we, who lost in stormy visions, keep
With phantoms an unprofitable strife,
And in mad trance, strike with our spirit's knife
Invulnerable nothings. *We* decay
Like corpses in a charnel; fear and grief
Convulse us and consume us day by day,
And cold hopes swarm like worms within our living clay.

He has outsoar'd the shadow of our night;
Envy and calumny and hate and pain,
And that unrest which men miscall delight,
Can touch him not and torture not again;
From the contagion of the world's slow stain
He is secure, and now can never mourn
A heart grown cold, a head grown gray in vain;
Nor, when the spirit's self has ceased to burn,
With sparkless ashes load an unlamented urn.

He lives, he wakes – 'tis Death is dead, not he;
Mourn not for Adonais. Thou young Dawn,
Turn all thy dew to splendour, for from thee
The spirit thou lamentest is not gone;
Ye caverns and ye forests, cease to moan!
Cease, ye faint flowers and fountains, and thou Air,
Which like a mourning veil thy scarf hadst thrown
O'er the abandon'd Earth, now leave it bare
Even to the joyous stars which smile on its despair!

He is made one with Nature: there is heard
His voice in all her music, from the moan
Of thunder, to the song of night's sweet bird;

He is a presence to be felt and known
In darkness and in light, from herb and stone,
Spreading itself where'er that Power may move
Which has withdrawn his being to its own;
Which wields the world with never-wearied love,
Sustains it from beneath, and kindles it above.

He is a portion of the loveliness
Which once he made more lovely . . .

PERCY BYSSHE SHELLEY (1792–1822)

The Reassurance

About ten days or so
After we saw you dead
You came back in a dream.
I'm all right now you said.

And it was you, although
You were fleshed out again:
You hugged us all round then,
And gave your welcoming beam.

How like you to be kind,
Seeking to reassure.
And, yes, how like my mind
To make itself secure.

THOM GUNN (1929–)

Transient Existence

This existence of ours is as transient as autumn clouds.
To watch the birth and death of beings is like looking
    at the movements of a dance.
A lifetime is like a flash of lightning in the sky,
Rushing by, like a torrent down a steep mountain.

BUDDHA (*c.* 560–480 BC)

Small Prayer

Change, move, dead clock, that this fresh day
May break with dazzling light to these sick eyes.
Burn, glare, old sun, so long unseen,
That time may find its sound again, and cleanse
Whatever it is that a wound remembers
After the healing ends.

WELDON KEES (1914–55)

Sea-Fever

I must go down to the seas again, to the lonely sea and the
    sky,
And all I ask is a tall ship and a star to steer her by,
And the wheel's kick and the wind's song and the white
    sail's shaking,
And a grey mist on the sea's face and a grey dawn breaking.

I must go down to the seas again, for the call of the
    running tide
Is a wild call and a clear call that may not be denied;
And all I ask is a windy day with the white clouds flying,
And the flung spray and the blown spume, and the sea-
    gulls crying.

I must go down to the seas again, to the vagrant gypsy life,
To the gull's way and the whale's way where the wind's like
    a whetted knife;
And all I ask is a merry yarn from a laughing fellow-rover,
And quiet sleep and a sweet dream when the long trick's
    over.

JOHN MASEFIELD (1878–1967)

from The Garden of Prosperine

From too much love of living,
   From hope and fear set free,
We thank with brief thanksgiving
   Whatever gods may be
That no life lives for ever;
That dead men rise up never;
That even the weariest river
   Winds somewhere safe to sea.

ALGERNON CHARLES SWINBURNE
(1837–1909)

Farewell, Sweet Dust

Now I have lost you, I must scatter
All of you on the air henceforth;
Not that to me it can ever matter
But it's only fair to the rest of earth

Now especially, when it is winter
And the sun's not half so bright as he was,
Who wouldn't be glad to find a splinter
That once was you, in the frozen grass?

Snowflakes, too, will be softer feathered,
Clouds, perhaps, will be whiter plumed;
Rain, whose brilliance you caught and gathered,
Purer silver have reassumed.

Farewell, sweet dust; I was never a miser:
Once, for a minute, I made you mine:
Now you are gone, I am none the wiser
But the leaves of the willow are bright as wine.

ELINOR WYLIE (1885–1928)

We'll Go No More A-roving

So, we'll go no more a-roving
So late into the night,
Though the heart be still as loving,
And the moon be still as bright.

For the sword outwears its sheath,
And the soul wears out the breast,
And the heart must pause to breathe,
And Love itself have rest.

Though the night was made for loving,
And the day returns too soon,
Yet we'll go no more a-roving
By the light of the moon.

LORD BYRON (1788–1824)

Requiescat

Strew on her roses, roses,
And never a spray of yew.
In quiet she reposes:
Ah! would that I did too.

Her mirth the world required:
She bathed it in smiles of glee.
But her heart was tired, tired,
And now they let her be.

Her life was turning, turning,
In mazes of heat and sound.
But for peace her soul was yearning,
And now peace laps her round.

Her cabin'd, ample Spirit,
It flutter'd and fail'd for breath.
To-night it doth inherit
The vasty Hall of Death.

MATTHEW ARNOLD (1822–88)

Crossing the Bar

Sunset and evening star,
    And one clear call for me!
And may there be no moaning of the bar,
    When I put out to sea,

But such a tide as moving seems asleep,
    Too full for sound and foam,
When that which drew from out the boundless deep
    Turns again home.

Twilight and evening bell,
    And after that the dark!
And may there be no sadness of farewell,
    When I embark;

For though from out our bourne of Time and Place
    The flood may bear me far,
I hope to see my Pilot face to face
    When I have crost the bar.

ALFRED, LORD TENNYSON (1809–92)

The Peace of Wild Things

When despair for the world grows in me
and I wake in the night at the least sound
in fear of what my life and my children's lives may be,
I go and lie down where the wood drake
rests in his beauty on the water, and the great heron feeds.
I come into the peace of wild things
who do not tax their lives with forethought
of grief. I come into the presence of still water.
And I feel above me the day-blind stars
waiting with their light. For a time
I rest in the grace of the world, and am free.

WENDELL BERRY (1934–)

Testament

'But how can I live without you?' she cried.

I left all the world to you when I died;
Beauty of earth and air and sea;
Leap of a swallow or a tree;
Kiss of rain and wind's embrace;
Passion of storm and winter's face;
Touch of feather, flower and stone;
Chiselled line of branch or bone;
Flight of stars, night's caravan;
Song of crickets – and of man –
All these I put in my testament,
All these I bequeathed you when I went.

'But how can I see them without your eyes
Or touch them without your hand?
How can I hear them without your ear,
Without your heart, understand?'

These too, these too, I leave to you!

ANNE MORROW LINDBERGH (1906–2001)

from Macbeth

ACT III, SCENE II

After life's fitful fever he sleeps well;
Treason has done his worst: nor steel, nor poison,
Malice domestic, foreign levy, nothing,
Can touch him further.

from Cymbeline

ACT IV, SCENE II

Fear no more the heat o' th' sun,
   Nor the furious winter's rages;
Thou thy worldly task hast done,
   Home art gone, and ta'en thy wages:
Golden lads and girls all must,
As chimney-sweepers, come to dust.

WILLIAM SHAKESPEARE (1564–1616)

from The Tempest

Our revels now are ended. These our actors,
As I foretold you, were all spirits, and
Are melted into air, into thin air:
And, like the baseless fabric of this vision,
The cloud-capp'd towers, the gorgeous palaces,
The solemn temples, the great globe itself,
Yea, all which it inherit, shall dissolve
And, like this insubstantial pageant faded,
Leave not a rack behind. We are such stuff
As dreams are made on, and our little life
Is rounded with a sleep.

WILLIAM SHAKESPEARE (1564–1616)

from a Letter to His Wife

Do not grieve for me too much. I am a spirit confident of my rights. Death is only an incident, & not the most important wh[ich] happens to us in this state of being. On the whole, especially since I met you my darling one I have been happy, & you have taught me how noble a woman's heart can be. If there is anywhere else I shall be on the look out for you. Meanwhile look forward, feel free, rejoice in Life, cherish the children, guard my memory. God bless you.

WINSTON CHURCHILL (1874–1965)

HYMNS, PRAYERS AND READINGS

The Lord's My Shepherd

PSALM 23

GOD'S PROVIDENCE

The Lord's my Shepherd, I'll not want;
    he makes me down to lie
in pastures green; he leadeth me
    the quiet waters by.

My soul he doth restore again,
    and me to walk doth make
within the paths of righteousness,
    e'en for his own name's sake.

Yea, though I walk through death's dark vale,
    yet will I fear none ill;
for thou art with me, and thy rod
    and staff me comfort still.

My table thou hast furnishèd
    in presence of my foes;
my head thou dost with oil anoint,
    and my cup overflows.

Goodness and mercy all my life
    shall surely follow me;
and in God's house for evermore
    my dwelling-place shall be.

SCOTTISH PSALTER, 1850

I Vow to Thee, My Country

I vow to thee, my country, all earthly things above,
entire and whole and perfect, the service of my love:
the love that asks no question, the love that stands the test,
that lays upon the altar the dearest and the best;
the love that never falters, the love that pays the price,
the love that makes undaunted the final sacrifice.

And there's another country, I've heard of long ago,
most dear to them that love her, most great to them that know;
we may not count her armies, we may not see her King;
her fortress is a faithful heart, her pride is suffering;
and soul by soul and silently her shining bounds increase,
and her ways are ways of gentleness and all her paths are peace.

CECIL SPRING-RICE (1859–1918)

Jerusalem

And did those feet in ancient time
   walk upon England's mountains green?
And was the holy Lamb of God
   on England's pleasant pastures seen?
And did the countenance divine
   shine forth upon our clouded hills?
And was Jerusalem builded here
   among those dark satanic mills?

Bring me my bow of burning gold!
   Bring me my arrows of desire!
Bring me my spear! O clouds, unfold!
   Bring me my chariot of fire!
I will not cease from mental fight,
   nor shall my sword sleep in my hand,
till we have built Jerusalem
   in England's green and pleasant land.

WILLIAM BLAKE (1757–1827)

Mine Eyes Have Seen the Glory
of the Coming of the Lord

Mine eyes have seen the glory of the coming of the Lord;
He is trampling out the vintage where the grapes of wrath are
      stored;
He hath loosed the fateful lightning of his terrible swift sword;
His truth is marching on.

   Glory! Glory! Hallelujah! Glory! Glory! Hallelujah!
   Glory! Glory! Hallelujah! Our God is marching on!

I have seen him in the watch-fires of a hundred circling camps;
They have builded him an altar in the evening dews and damps;
I have read his righteous sentence by the dim and flaring lamps:
His day is marching on.

   Glory! Glory! Hallelujah! . . .

I have read a fiery gospel, writ in burnished rows of steel:
'As ye deal with my contemners, so with you my grace shall
      deal';
Let the Hero born of woman crush the serpent with his heel,
Since God is marching on.

   Glory! Glory! Hallelujah! . . .

He has sounded forth the trumpet that shall never call retreat;
He is sifting out the hearts of men before his judgement seat;
O, be swift, my soul, to answer him; be jubilant my feet!
Our God is marching on.

   Glory! Glory! Hallelujah! . . .

In the beauty of the lilies Christ was born across the sea,
With a glory in his bosom that transfigures you and me;

As he died to make men holy, let us die to make men free,
While God is marching on.

Glory! Glory! Hallelujah! . . .

He is coming like the glory of the morning on the wave;
He is wisdom to the mighty, he is succour to the brave;
So the world shall be his footstool, and the soul of time his
      slave,
Our God is marching on.

Glory! Glory! Hallelujah! . . .

JULIA WARD HOWE (1819–1910)

from Lord of the Dance

I danced in the morning
When the world was begun,
And I danced in the moon
And the stars and the sun,
And I came down from heaven
And I danced on the earth,
At Bethlehem
I had my birth.

Dance, then, wherever you may be,
I am the Lord of the Dance, said he,
And I'll lead you all, wherever you may be,
And I'll lead you all in the Dance, said he.

I danced on a Friday
When the sky turned black —
It's hard to dance
With the devil on your back.
They buried my body
And they thought I'd gone,
But I am the dance,
And I still go on.

They cut me down
And I leapt up high;
I am the life
That'll never, never die;
I'll live in you
If you'll live in me —
I am the Lord
Of the Dance, said he.

SYDNEY CARTER (1915–)

Amazing Grace

Amazing grace! how sweet the sound
    That saved a wretch like me!
I once was lost, but now am found,
    Was blind, but now I see.

'Twas grace that taught my heart to fear,
    And grace my fears relieved;
How precious did that grace appear
    The hour I first believed.

Through many dangers, toils, and snares
    I have already come;
'Tis grace hath brought me safe thus far,
    And grace will lead me home.

The Lord has promised good to me,
    His word my hope secures;
He will my shield and portion be
    As long as life endures.

JOHN NEWTON (1725–1807)

Abide with Me

Abide with me; fast falls the eventide:
the darkness deepens; Lord, with me abide:
when other helpers fail, and comforts flee,
help of the helpless, O abide with me.

Swift to its close ebbs out life's little day;
earth's joys grow dim, its glories pass away;
change and decay in all around I see:
O thou who changest not, abide with me.

I need thy presence every passing hour;
what but thy grace can foil the tempter's power?
Who like thyself my guide and stay can be?
Through cloud and sunshine, Lord, abide with me.

I fear no foe with thee at hand to bless;
ills have no weight, and tears no bitterness.
Where is death's sting? Where, grave, thy victory?
I triumph still, if thou abide with me.

Hold thou thy cross before my closing eyes;
shine through the gloom, and point me to the skies:
heaven's morning breaks, and earth's vain shadows flee;
in life, in death, O Lord, abide with me.

Henry Francis Lyte (1793–1847)

Immortal, Invisible, God Only Wise

Immortal, invisible, God only wise,
in light inaccessible hid from our eyes,
most blessèd, most glorious, the Ancient of Days,
almighty, victorious, thy great name we praise.

Unresting, unhasting, and silent as light,
nor wanting, nor wasting, thou rulest in might;
thy justice like mountains high soaring above
thy clouds which are fountains of goodness and love.

To all life thou givest, to both great and small;
in all life thou livest, the true life of all;
we blossom and flourish as leaves on the tree,
and wither and perish; but naught changeth thee.

Great Father of glory, pure Father of light,
thine angels adore thee, all veiling their sight;
all laud we would render: O help us to see
'tis only the splendour of light hideth thee.

WALTER CHALMERS SMITH (1824–1908)

All Things Bright and Beautiful

All things bright and beautiful,
*   all creatures great and small,*
all things wise and wonderful,
*   the Lord God made them all.*

Each little flower that opens,
    each little bird that sings,
he made their glowing colours,
    he made their tiny wings:

The purple-headed mountain,
    the river running by,
the sunset, and the morning
    that brightens up the sky:

The cold wind in the winter,
    the pleasant summer sun,
the ripe fruits in the garden,
    he made them every one:

The tall trees in the greenwood,
    the meadows where we play,
the rushes by the water
    we gather every day:

He gave us eyes to see them,
    and lips that we might tell
how great is God almighty,
    who has made all things well:

All things bright and beautiful,
*   all creatures great and small,*
all things wise and wonderful,
*   the Lord God made them all.*

CECIL ALEXANDER (1818–95)

Swing Low, Sweet Chariot

Swing low, sweet chariot
Comin' for to carry me home;
Swing low, sweet chariot
Comin' for to carry me home.

I looked over Jordan, and what did I see,
Comin' for to carry me home?
A band of angels comin' after me,
Comin' for to carry me home.

Swing low, sweet chariot,
Comin' for to carry me home;
Swing low, sweet chariot,
Comin' for to carry me home.

If you get there before I do,
Comin' for to carry me home,
Tell all my friends I'm comin' too,
Comin' for to carry me home.

Swing low, sweet chariot,
Comin' for to carry me home;
Swing low, sweet chariot,
Comin' for to carry me home.

Sometimes I'm up, sometimes I'm down,
Comin' for to carry me home;
Yet still my soul feels heavn'ly bound,
Comin' for to carry me home.

Swing low, sweet chariot,
Comin' for to carry me home;
Swing low, sweet chariot,
Comin' for to carry me home.

AFRICAN–AMERICAN SPIRITUAL

The Eternal Goodness

Within the maddening maze of things
And toss'd by storm and flood,
To one fixed trust my spring clings,
I know that God is good.

I know not what the future hath
Of marvel or surprise;
Assured alone that life and death
His mercy underlies.

And so beside the silent sea
I wait the muffled oar;
No harm from Him can come to me
On ocean or on shore.

I know not where His islands lift
Their fronded palms in air,
I only know I cannot drift
Beyond His love and care.

And Thou, O Lord, by whom are seen
Thy creatures as they be,
Forgive me if too close I lean
My human heart on Thee.

JOHN GREENLEAF WHITTIER (1807–92)

Lord of All Hopefulness

Lord of all hopefulness, Lord of all joy,
whose trust, ever childlike, no cares could destroy,
be there at our waking, and give us, we pray,
your bliss in our hearts, Lord, at the break of the day.

Lord of all eagerness, Lord of all faith,
whose strong hands were skilled at the plane and the lathe,
be there at our labours, and give us, we pray,
your strength in our hearts, Lord, at the noon of the day.

Lord of all kindliness, Lord of all grace,
your hands swift to welcome, your arms to embrace,
be there at our homing, and give us, we pray,
your love in our hearts, Lord, at the eve of the day.

Lord of all gentleness, Lord of all calm,
whose voice is contentment, whose presence is balm,
be there at our sleeping, and give us, we pray,
your peace in our hearts, Lord, at the end of the day.

JAN STRUTHER (1901–53)

Let Us Now Praise Famous Men

Let us now praise famous men, and our fathers that begat us. The Lord hath wrought great glory by them through his great power from the beginning. Such as did bear rule in their kingdoms, men renowned for their power, giving counsel by their understanding, and declaring prophecies: Leaders of the people by their counsels, and by their knowledge of learning meet for the people, wise and eloquent in their instructions: such as found out musical tunes, and recited verses in writing: rich men furnished with ability, living peaceably in their habitations: all these were honoured in their generations, and were the glory of their times. There be of them, that have left a name behind them, that their praises might be reported. And some there be, which have no memorial; who are perished, as though they had never been; and are become as though they had never been born; and their children after them. But these were merciful men, whose righteousness hath not been forgotten. With their seed shall continually remain a good inheritance, and their children are within the covenant. Their seed standeth fast, and their children for their sakes. Their seed shall remain for ever, and their glory shall not be blotted out. Their bodies are buried in peace; but their name liveth for evermore.

ECCLESIASTICUS, 44, 1–14

And I Saw a New Heaven

And I saw a new heaven and a new earth: for the first heaven and the first earth were passed away; and there was no more sea. And I John saw the holy city, new Jerusalem, coming down from God out of heaven, prepared as a bride adorned for her husband. And I heard a great voice out of heaven saying, Behold, the tabernacle of God is with men, and he will dwell with them, and they shall be his people, and God himself shall be with them, and be their God. And God shall wipe away all tears from their eyes; and there shall be no more death, neither sorrow, nor crying, neither shall there be any more pain: for the former things are passed away. And he that sat upon the throne said, Behold, I make all things new. And he said unto me, Write: for these words are true and faithful. And he said unto me, It is done. I am Alpha and Omega, the beginning and the end. I will give unto him that is athirst of the fountain of the water of life freely. He that overcometh shall inherit all things; and I will be his God, and he shall be my son.

REVELATION, 21: 1–7

In the Beginning Was the Word

In the beginning was the Word, and the Word was with God, and the Word was God. The same was in the beginning with God. All things were made by him; and without him was not any thing made that was made. In him was life; and the life was the light of men. And the light shineth in darkness; and the darkness comprehended it not.

There was a man sent from God, whose name was John. The same came for a witness, to bear witness of the Light, that all men through him might believe. He was not that Light, but was sent to bear witness of that Light. That was the true Light, which lighteth every man that cometh into the world. He was in the world, and the world was made by him, and the world knew him not. He came unto his own, and his own received him not. But as many as received him, to them gave he power to become the sons of God, even to them that believe on his name: which were born, not of blood, nor of the will of the flesh, nor of the will of man, but of God. And the Word was made flesh, and dwelt among us, (and we beheld his glory, the glory as of the only begotten of the Father), full of grace and truth.

St John 1: 1–14

I Will Lift Up Mine Eyes Unto the Hills

A SONG OF DEGREES

I will lift up mine eyes unto the hills, from whence cometh
    my help.
My help cometh from the Lord, which made heaven and earth.
He will not suffer thy foot to be moved: he that keepeth thee
    will not slumber.
Behold, he that keepeth Israel shall neither slumber nor sleep.
The Lord is thy keeper: the Lord is thy shade upon thy right
    hand.
The sun shall not smite thee by day, nor the moon by night.
The Lord shall preserve thee from all evil: he shall preserve thy
    soul.
The Lord shall preserve thy going out and thy coming in from
    this time forth, and even for evermore.

PSALM 121

For Those Who Mourn

Almighty God, Father of all mercies and giver of all comfort: deal graciously, we pray thee, with those who mourn, that casting every care on thee, they may know the consolation of thy love; through Jesus Christ our Lord. Amen.

EPISCOPAL BOOK OF COMMON PRAYER

New Freshness

Holy Spirit, Spirit of the Living God,
you breathe in us
on all that is inadequate and fragile.

You make living water spring even
from our hurts themselves. And
through you, the valley of tears
becomes a place of wellsprings.

So, in an inner life
with neither beginning nor end,
your continual presence
makes new freshness break through. Amen.

BROTHER ROGER OF TAIZÉ (1915–)

Look Up

I would be true for there are those who trust me,
I would be pure for there are those who care,
I would be strong for there is much to suffer,
I would be brave for there is much to dare,
I would be friend of all, the foe, the friendless,
I would be giving and forget the gift,
I would be humble for I know my weakness,
I would look up, and laugh, and love, and live.

ANONYMOUS

For Those Whom We Love

O Father of all, we pray to thee for those whom we love, but see no longer. Grant them thy peace; let light perpetual shine upon them; and in thy loving wisdom and almighty power work in them the good purpose of thy perfect will; through Jesus Christ our Lord. Amen.

EPISCOPAL BOOK OF COMMON PRAYER

No Ends, No Beginnings

Bring us, O Lord God, at our last awakening into the house and gate of heaven; to enter into that gate and dwell in that house, where there shall be no darkness nor dazzling, but one equal light; no noise nor silence, but one equal music; no fears nor hopes, but one equal possession; no ends, nor beginnings, but one equal eternity; in the habitations of thy glory and dominion, world without end. Amen.

JOHN DONNE (1572–1631)

Death Is Only an Horizon

O God, who holdest all souls in life and callest them unto thee as seemeth best: we give them back, dear God, to thee who gavest them to us. But as thou didst not lose them in the giving, so we do not lose them by their return. For not as the world giveth, givest thou, O Lord of souls: that which thou givest thou takest away: for life is eternal, and love is immortal, and death is only the horizon, and the horizon is nothing save the limit of our sight.

ROSSITER W. RAYMOND (1840–1918)

from The Bhagavad Gita

CHAPTER 4

In any way that men love me, in that same way they find my love: for many are the paths of men, but they all in the end come to me.

ANONYMOUS

Acknowledgements

Many thanks to all those who have offered suggestions, including my mother Ceris Emerson, always my help and support, Valerie Grove, Gayle Hunnicutt, Anthony Holden, Canon David Meara of St Bride's, Fleet Street, and, in particular, the late Giles Gordon. Thanks also to Jill Foulston, Connie Hallam and Viv Redman.

The publishers would like to acknowledge the following for permission to reproduce copyright material:

Extracts from *The Authorized Version of The Bible* (*The King James Bible*) and from *The Book of Common Prayer* (1928), the rights of which are vested in the Crown, are reproduced by permission of the Crown's Patentee, Cambridge University Press.

Extract from 'Song of Songs' from *The New English Bible*, copyright © Oxford University Press and Cambridge University Press 1961, 1970, reproduced by permission of Cambridge University Press.

Akahito translated by Kenneth Rexroth: 'Memory Does Not Pass Away' from *One Hundred Poems from the Japanese* (New Directions, 1955), copyright © 1955 New Directions Publishing Corp., reprinted by permission of the publisher.

W. H. Auden: 'Twelve Songs IX' ('Funeral Blues'), and 'Musée des Beaux Arts', from *Collected Shorter Poems, 1927–1957* (1976), reprinted by permission of the publishers, Faber & Faber Ltd.

Marcus Aurelius: extract from *The Meditations of the Emperor Marcus Aurelius Antonius* translated by A. S. L. Farquharson (OUP, 1944), reprinted by permission of Oxford University Press.

Louis de Bernières: extract from *Captain Corelli's Mandolin* (Secker & Warburg, 1994), reprinted by permission of The Random House Group Ltd.

Wendell Berry: 'The Peace of Wild Things' from *Collected Poems: 1957–1982* (North Point Press, 1985), copyright © 1985 by Wendell Berry, reprinted by permission of North Point Press, a division of Farrar, Straus & Giroux, LLC.

The Bhagavad Gita: verses translated by Juan Mascaro (Penguin Classics, 1962) copyright © Juan Mascaro 1962, reprinted by permission of Penguin Books Ltd.

Laurence Binyon: 'For the Fallen (September 1914)' from *Collected Poems 1869–1943*, 2 vols. (Macmillan, 1943), reprinted by permission of the Society of Authors as the Literary Representative of the Estate of Laurence Binyon.

Jorge Luis Borges: extract from 'Delia Elena San Marco' in *Dreamtigers* translated by Mildred Boyer and Harold Morland (University of Texas Press, 1964), copyright © 1964, renewed 1992, reprinted by permission of the University of Texas Press.

George Mackay Brown: 'Elegy "In Memoriam IK"' from *The Wreck of the Archangel* (1989), reprinted by permission of John Murray (Publishers).

Penelope Lively: extract from *Perfect Happiness* (Heinemann, 1983), reprinted by permission of David Higham Associates.

Norman McCaig: 'Praise of a Man' from *Collected Poems* (Chatto & Windus, 1990), reprinted by permission of The Random House Group Ltd.

Ian McEwan: extract from *The Child in Time* (Cape, 1987), reprinted by permission of The Random House Group Ltd; extract from 'Only Love and then Oblivion: Love Was All They Had to Set Against Their Murderers', copyright © Ian McEwan 2001, *The Guardian*, 25. 9. 01, reprinted by permission of the author c/o Rogers, Coleridge & White Ltd, 20 Powis Mews, London W11 1JN

John Gillespie Magee: 'High Flight (An Airman's Ecstasy)' from *John Magee, the Pilot Poet* (This England, 1996), reprinted by permission of This England Books, Cheltenham.

Leo Marks: 'Code Poem for the French Resistance' from *Between Silk and Cyanide: The Codebreakers War*, copyright © Leo Marks 1999, reprinted by permission of HarperCollins Publishers Ltd.

John Masefield: 'Sea Fever' from *Collected Poems* (Heinemann, 1923), reprinted by permission of the Society of Authors as the Literary Representative of the Estate of John Masefield.

Mei Yao Ch'en translated by Kenneth Rexroth: 'In Broad Daylight I Dream of my Dead Wife' from *One Hundred Poems from the Chinese* (New Directions, 1971), copyright © 1971 Kenneth Rexroth, reprinted by permission of New Directions Publishing Corp.

Edna St Vincent Millay: 'Dirge without Music', and 'Time Does Not Bring Relief' from *Collected Poems* (HarperCollins), copyright © 1917, 1923, 1945, 1951 by Edna St Vincent Millay and Norma Millay Ellis, reprinted by permission of Elizabeth Barnett, Literary Executor. All rights reserved.

Index of First Lines

Index of Authors

BE MINE
Sally Emerson

Be Mine is a collection of poetry and prose for lovers. Selected by author Sally Emerson, this delightful and provocative anthology brings together some of the world's most beautiful love poems and readings, both comic and profound. The perfect partner for weddings and valentines, anniversaries and vow renewals, for ceremonies civil or religious, above all it will be enjoyed by anyone who wants to understand the great mysteries of love.

Be Mine charts and celebrates all stages of romance: from first loves to lasting loves, from proposals to weddings to wrong turnings and happy endings. Here are songs from musicals, from Lennon & McCartney, extracts from films, amusing old letters of proposal. Read the love poems of Betjeman, Shakespeare, Donne, Pablo Neruda, Margaret Atwood, Wendy Cope. Note Nietszche on the ingredient that makes a happy marriage, Einstein on the tragedy of marriage, the girls from *Guys and Dolls* on marrying the man today and changing his ways tomorrow.

This is a rollicking, acute, varied anthology that will make you think and feel on every page. It is in essence an exploration of that elusive quality and how it changes and grows – a journey through the epic and domestic, the patience and passions of love.

A Little, Brown Original

978-0-316-73258-1

£14.99